P9-DHN-276

Clara stared at Alaric.

Did he just say "married"?

"What?"

"Married."

Yes, he did.

She blinked a couple of times, her brain grasping for a response. It finally settled on "Why?"

His icy smile disappeared, replaced by a quelling glance that all but shouted how foolish she was for not immediately realizing where he was going with this.

"You're carrying the heir to the Linnaean throne."

Her eyes drifted back down to the test. Over twelve hours had passed since her suspicions had been confirmed and it still didn't seem real. She'd caught herself glancing at her reflection more than once as she'd moved throughout the day. But no matter how many times she'd looked, her belly had remained flat, her body showing no outward signs that a child was growing inside her.

"And?"

Alaric's muscles tightened, the material of his suit sleeves stretching across his biceps.

"And I will be damned before I allow my child to be born out of wedlock and see his or her legacy tainted by scandal."

The Van Ambrose Royals

With this convenient royal ring...

The Mediterranean kingdom of Linnaea is a nation in trouble, ruled by tyrannical, hedonistic King Daxon, who cares nothing for his people or the throne. But change is coming!

Crown Prince Alaric and long-lost Princess Briony are proudly determined to undo their father's mistakes and restore Linnaea to its former glory.

But for now, there's something that requires their more immediate attention... Being conveniently bound to perfect royal partners. With a passion that shocks—*and thrills*—them both!

Discover Briony's story in
A Cinderella for the Prince's Revenge

Read Alaric's story
The Prince's Pregnant Secretary

Both available now!

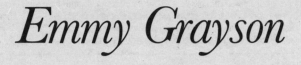

Emmy Grayson

THE PRINCE'S PREGNANT SECRETARY

If you purchased this book without a cover you should be aware that this book is stolen property. It was reported as "unsold and destroyed" to the publisher, and neither the author nor the publisher has received any payment for this "stripped book."

Recycling programs for this product may not exist in your area.

ISBN-13: 978-1-335-73880-6

The Prince's Pregnant Secretary

Copyright © 2022 by Emmy Grayson

All rights reserved. No part of this book may be used or reproduced in any manner whatsoever without written permission except in the case of brief quotations embodied in critical articles and reviews.

This is a work of fiction. Names, characters, places and incidents are either the product of the author's imagination or are used fictitiously. Any resemblance to actual persons, living or dead, businesses, companies, events or locales is entirely coincidental.

For questions and comments about the quality of this book, please contact us at CustomerService@Harlequin.com.

Harlequin Enterprises ULC
22 Adelaide St. West, 41st Floor
Toronto, Ontario M5H 4E3, Canada
www.Harlequin.com

Printed in U.S.A.

Emmy Grayson wrote her first book at the age of seven about a spooky ghost. Her passion for romance novels began a few years later with the discovery of a worn copy of Kathleen Woodiwiss's *A Rose in Winter* buried on her mother's bookshelf. She lives in the Midwest countryside with her husband (who's also her ex-husband), their baby boy and enough animals to start their own zoo.

Books by Emmy Grayson

Harlequin Presents

The Infamous Cabrera Brothers

His Billion-Dollar Takeover Temptation
Proof of Their One Hot Night
A Deal for the Tycoon's Diamonds

The Van Ambrose Royals

A Cinderella for the Prince's Revenge

Visit the Author Profile page at Harlequin.com.

For my husband, always.

For Mom, Dad and Mama Pam, for always believing in me.

For Nate and Kels, for listening to me panic and supporting me during Deadline Week.

For Katelyn, Teddy and Laura, friends and fellow writers who helped bring Clara to life.

CHAPTER ONE

THE FURY BURNING through Prince Alaric Van Ambrose's veins surprised him with its intensity. He hadn't thought it possible to experience this level of anger unless it involved his useless sire.

But it wasn't his father staring up at him from the picture pulled up on Clara's tablet. No, it was his ex-fiancée, Celestine Osborne, in the arms of not one but two men on the dance floor of some ritzy New York club. One man had his hands on her waist, his hips pressed provocatively against her barely covered rear. The other man's hands rested just beneath the curves of her breasts, which nearly popped out of her plunging halter top.

Most women in that position would have been focusing on at least one of their admirers, perhaps even ducking away from the bright flash of the camera.

Celestine, however, had looked straight at the photographer, her tawny gold eyes defiant, her perfectly shaped chin raised as she smiled smugly. Some might find her apparent confidence sexy. But to him, her bared pearly white teeth reminded him of a piranha.

Slowly, he uncurled his fingers from around his

phone and set it on his desk. He'd kept the photo pulled up when he'd called Celestine, a visual reminder to himself that he could no longer overlook her scandalous behavior. Their engagement of nine years had been a business agreement arranged by their fathers, but one he thought they'd both willingly entered into.

Except according to her and the acrimonious conversation that had ended with her screaming at him before terminating their engagement, marrying him had been the last thing she'd ever wanted.

What did it say that he was angrier that he'd wasted so many years waiting on Celestine and having her antics associated with the country he was trying to rebuild than mourning the loss of his future wife?

"I'm sorry, Your Highness."

Clara's cool voice soothed some of the tension tightening his neck. She had been his executive assistant for the past seven years. Dependable, professional and talented with words, she'd made herself indispensable.

But over the last year, whether it was the escalating tension with his father, the increasing audacity of Celestine's behavior or terminating his last affair with a Spanish oil heiress, something had changed. He'd found himself seeking her out more, asking for her opinion on government matters, enjoying her company.

Red flags. She was his employee, and he was engaged.

Was, whispered the devil on his shoulder as he looked up to see her approaching his desk. It didn't help that Clara was a beautiful woman. Usually, she wore pant or skirt suits, form-fitting enough to be professional but loose enough that he could easily dismiss thoughts that started to take on an inappropriate nature.

But tonight…tonight she wore a deep blue gown that reminded him of the North Sea just before the sun rose. The way the material wrapped around her slender body, clinging to her slight curves before cascading down into a swirl of silk around her feet, sent a bolt of forbidden desire through his body. Her pale blond hair, normally wrapped in a tight bun at the base of her neck, had been pulled up into an elegant twist with soft curls framing her elfin face.

She reached over and tapped something on the tablet. Celestine's arrogant expression, simultaneously lewd and immature, disappeared.

"I'm not sorry." He leaned back in his chair and scrubbed a hand over his face. "Actually, I am. I'm sorry that I didn't have this confrontation sooner. Linnaea deserves better from its future queen."

Clara's lips parted for a moment, then compressed together in a firm line. He arched a brow.

"What?"

"It's not my place to say."

He chuckled. Rarely did he let his guard down, but with Clara, it had become easy to do. The woman didn't pull punches. He always knew where he stood with her, and he also knew that she had both his and Linnaea's best interests at heart.

"When has that ever stopped you from saying exactly what's on your mind?"

The corner of her mouth slid up as something akin to a sparkle danced in her eyes.

A sparkle? Really?

"You deserve better, too, Your Highness."

The sentiment tugged at his chest and catapulted him back to that night eleven months ago when she'd said almost the exact same thing. When, if he was being honest with himself, things had started to change between them, at least on his end.

He stood and stalked over to the floor-to-ceiling window behind his desk. The lake glittered silver beneath the light of the frost moon. Snow had covered the ground since late October, dressing Linnaea's spectacular scenery in a veil of white.

There were two things Alaric had loved in his life; his late mother, Marianne, and his country. It had been because of his love for Linnaea that he'd agreed to the engagement with Celestine in the first place.

A bird soared across the lake, dappled white wings spread against the night sky. An eagle owl, judging by the wingspan. It dipped toward the water before lazily drifting back up toward the stars. He envied the owl's languid pace, no schedule, committees or legislation to keep it chained to a desk.

No errant fiancées, either, constantly threatening what he'd worked so hard for since he was sixteen, old enough to realize that if anyone was going to save Linnaea, it sure as hell wasn't his father, Daxon Van Ambrose. Daxon liked the title of king well enough; he just didn't want to do the hard work that came with it, preferring to spend as if he had endless resources at his fingertips instead of the country's dwindling treasury. The primary reason why Alaric had agreed to an engagement with a woman he'd never seen.

Nine years. Nine years since he'd met Celestine and

her real estate tycoon father before he had signed the contract agreeing to give Max Osborne the one thing his billions couldn't buy: a royal title. The contract allowed for up to ten years for the marriage to take place, with Max pumping money into Linnaea's economy through various projects until Celestine officially became a Van Ambrose. After the marriage, a dowry consisting of a couple billion dollars would appear.

He'd sold the role of queen to the highest bidder.

The target of his anger shifted from Celestine to himself. He'd been the one to agree to his father and Max's ridiculous contract. He'd been twenty-six and already as involved as Daxon would allow him to be in Linnaea's operations. Celestine had been all of nineteen, barely out of school and entertaining wide-eyed fantasies of being a princess. The moment he'd met her in the palace throne room, a little-used elegant hall Daxon had picked to impress his audience, he'd known she was too young to fully understand what she was agreeing to.

But he'd signed. He'd signed the contract and sold not only his soul but that of a young woman to two devils who cared more about their own interests than the well-being of a country.

The picture from the club flashed in his mind again. He might have made a mistake nine years ago, but Celestine had made her own choices in that time. Her behavior had grown increasingly erratic, the tabloid features more embarrassing, especially since she'd quit college.

When she'd answered the phone, her groggy voice had quickly sharpened into a razor blade as she'd asked if he was calling to be a "stick-in-the-mud." He'd told her he was done, that either she cease her partying and set a wedding date or he would call her father to renegotiate. She'd responded with four words: "Go ahead. I'm done."

A different kind of tension tightened his back. He kept his eyes trained on the mountain peaks beyond the lake. A familiar, dependable sight. Better to focus on that than the heightened awareness of his secretary.

Executive assistant, he acknowledged internally with a slight quirk of his lips. Clara despised being called "secretary."

"I'm a prince, Clara. Not a hero in a fairy tale. The engagement was never about love or even compatibility. It's always been about money."

He spat the last word out. He'd spent his entire life fighting to distance himself from his father's legacy of womanizing, drinking and spending what little wealth Linnaea had.

Yet here he was, obsessing over money. That one of his first thoughts had been satisfaction that, because Celestine had been the one to break the engagement, Linnaea would still receive a handsome payout from Osborne Construction, said enough about who he had become and what his priorities were. He'd almost dragged a very reluctant bride to the altar for her fortune.

Revulsion rippled through him.

"I've prepared an initial statement for your approval—"

"Send it."

He felt more than heard her huff.

"I need your approval."

"Granted."

A louder sigh.

"That's not how this works, Your Highness."

The quelling glance he delivered over his shoulder didn't stop Clara's determined march across the room. The closer she got, the tauter his muscles grew.

She stopped next to him and handed him the tablet, a document now replacing Celestine's photo. He focused on the black-and-white text. Better that than the tantalizing floral sweetness teasing him.

Prince Alaric Van Ambrose and Miss Celestine Osborne have announced they are no longer engaged. They wish each other the best...

His lips twisted. Celestine's voice, shrill and frazzled, echoed in his ears. Somehow her screaming that she wouldn't be caught dead in a marriage to a stonecold bastard or stuck living in a frozen backwater country didn't align with "wishing him the best."

"Fine."

The tablet disappeared. Clara, unfortunately, didn't. Out of the corner of his eye, he saw her attention drop down to the tablet as she tapped something out. The glow of the screen lit her delicate profile.

He knew the exact moment Clara had gone from being trusted employee and confidant to something more. Someone he could depend on, someone he looked forward to seeing.

The first few years of their engagement, Alaric had kept his distance from his fiancée. Celestine had seemed so young. Neither of them had been in a rush to get married, not while Max's construction projects finally flooded some much-needed cash and prestige into Linnaea. Clara had told him after the signing of the contract that she intended to live the next few years as she saw fit, including dating. Given that he'd known her for less than an hour, he'd been all too glad to agree.

Idiot.

While he'd been busy building up Linnaea behind the scenes and indulging in the occasional discreet affair, Celestine had started to act out, each year getting worse and worse as they neared the end of the engagement period. The last couple of years, he'd ceased his romantic involvements and tried to get to know his future wife better. He'd despised what he saw: a pampered, spoiled heiress who could have done anything with her life and instead chose to overindulge in the same manner his father did.

But he was not going to go back on his word or risk Linnaea's financial future.

It was why a year ago, the day before the annual Christmas Eve ball at the palace, he'd sought solace in his private gym downstairs when Celestine had shown up to a dinner with Linnaea's top officials already tipsy and wearing a dress better described as a shirt given how little it covered.

He'd made it through that dinner. Barely. A guard had escorted Celestine to her room after dessert, not allowing her the opportunity to join the party in after-dinner drinks and further embarrass herself and him. He'd made his excuses, ignoring the mix of pity and condescension, and sought solace in the small gym in the depths of the palace. He'd been in the middle of beating the hell out of a punching bag, wearing nothing but sweatpants with perspiration pouring down his back, when Clara had walked in. He hadn't let up, for

once not caring that he wasn't being seen in a princely
light. Who cared about how people saw him when the
future queen of Linnaea was making an ass of herself
just a few floors above?

She hadn't run away screaming. She hadn't chas-
tised him for leaving the dinner. No, she'd sat down on
a weight bench in all of her evening finery, clasped her
hands in her lap and asked if he wanted to talk about it.

He hadn't. Hence the punching bag. But for the first
time in years, someone had cared. When he'd growled
that he'd rather be left alone, she'd given him a smile
tinged with sadness before getting up and heading for
the door. It had pissed him off. He didn't want her pity,
and he'd said so.

The gentle tinkling of her laughter still rippled across
his skin.

*You are not one to be pitied, Your Highness. You
just deserve better.*

"Sent."

"Thank you, Clara."

Her eyes moved up, then fastened on the owl as it
continued its journey toward the pine forest on the south
side of the lake. A smile crossed her face.

"Hard to believe that I live here sometimes."

The awe in her voice made his heart squeeze in his
chest. He had yet to find someone else who loved his
country as much as he did, but Clara came a very close
second.

"Oh?"

"Linnaea's like a fairy tale."

The huskiness in her voice, tinged with a wistfulness
he hadn't heard before, heated his blood. He'd done a

damn good job keeping whatever emotions she'd stirred up under wraps, told himself it was the stress and lack of female companionship.

But when she talked like that, when he heard the mutual admiration in her tone and saw the happiness that softened her face and revealed her true beauty behind the efficient facade she wore so often, he found himself barely keeping his hands off her.

"Fairy tales usually have happy endings."

"Not the originals." Clara chuckled. "The originals were quite ghastly. Lots of blood and executions."

Alaric arched an eyebrow. Normally their conversations revolved around legislation or current events.

"When my father finds out his contract with Max Osborne is no more, there could very well be an execution in Linnaea's future."

He bit back a smile at Clara's unladylike smile.

"Your sister's marriage will bring money to Linnaea. And the Swiss ambassador just said he's willing to advocate for an alliance." She gently nudged him with her shoulder, a break from protocol that made electricity shoot across his skin. "Because of everything you've done, Your Highness."

He wanted to accept the rosy picture Clara was offering him. Discovering he had a long-lost half sister had been surprising but not a shock given his father's numerous affairs over the years. Really, the bigger shock was that weren't more by-blows running around. Briony had entered into a marital contract with Cassius Adama, a Linnaean who hadn't let his banishment from his home country stop him from accumulating his own fortune or his own royal title. Alaric had been against the arranged engagement from the start. There had been too many parallels between the arrangement his father had made with Max Osborn. He still didn't fully trust the younger man, but based on what he'd observed the last few weeks, Cass appeared to truly care for his sister. And Briony had impressed him with how quickly she'd not only adapted to royal life, but thrown herself into advocating for the downtrodden people of her new country.

There had been plenty of unexpected positive developments in the last few weeks. But that didn't mean there wouldn't be hell to pay, both with King Daxon Van Ambrose and Celestine's father, Max. Yes, Briony and Cass's marriage, coupled with the foreign support, would get Linnaea closer to the financial independence he'd been working so hard for. Still, Celestine's money would have gotten them even closer.

"Have you always been a secret optimist? Or is the situation that bad that you feel the need to give me a pep talk?"

This time her chuckle carried an edge, one that hinted at darker things in Clara Stephenson's past.

"Most definitely not an optimist. I prefer to think of myself as a realist." She gestured toward the window. "But even a realist can be moved by this."

That floral scent, hints of rose and sweetness and just a touch of spice, wrapped around him and wound a spell that lit the match and started a fire burning low in his gut. A fire that demanded he lift the curls lying so gently on her swanlike neck, press his lips to her skin and finally taste her before he went mad.

He needed to put distance between them. Now.

He started to turn away. A delicate pressure on his arm stopped him, rooted his feet to the ground as his body went rock hard.

Don't look. Don't look.

He wasn't thinking straight. Couldn't think straight with finding out he had a long-lost sister, entering into her own royal agreement with her new fiancé, having his own fiancée break up with him and continuing to put up with Daxon's antics. He was wound so tight that anything could set him off.

Could make him do things he shouldn't do.

"It will be okay, Alaric."

It was the use of his name that made him look, the first time he'd heard it on her lips. The sound of it charged the air around them, tension crackling as the rest of the world faded away at the sight of her pale hand resting against his black sleeve.

"Clara…"

His voice came out a growl, raw and on the verge of doing something very unprincely. It should have made her yank her hand away and run for the door.

Instead, her fingers tightened on his sleeve. Her sharp inhale echoed like a gunshot in the room.

Then he looked up, met those arctic-blue eyes with his own gaze, and the world burned.

Did he move first? Did she? Or did they both just crash into each other at the speed of light? One moment they were staring at each other, awareness washing over them in waves and drowning them in lust. The next their bodies were pressed together so tightly he didn't even breathe before his hands slid into her silky hair and held her in place as he slanted his lips across hers.

It wasn't a gentle, courtly kiss. It wasn't romantic. It was hard, possessive, almost punishing, as if to show her the animal he'd always feared he secretly was beneath the controlled exterior he presented to the world.

Like your father.

Then her hands came up and cupped his face, cool and gentle, soothing some of the angry passion smoldering in his chest. It didn't stop him from running his tongue along the seam of her mouth and invading when her lips parted for him. But it did stop him from flinging her away and ordering her to leave before he did something even more stupid.

Something like let his hands move from her hair, now tumbling in a blond mass of curls down her back to her waist, and pull her hips against his. Something like deepening the kiss when she moaned into his mouth and arched her lithe body against him.

The thinnest thread of sanity broke through. It gave him just enough power to pull back, to rest his forehead against hers as his chest heaved.

"Clara, we —"

Her hands rested on his chest, her touch searing him straight through the thin fabric of his dress shirt.

"Alaric."

The raw need in her voice made his grip tighten.

"Don't stop."

Had he thought he was on fire before? Because it was nothing compared to the inferno that blazed forth and scorched all rational thought at her words. He scooped her up in his arms, planting another soul-searing kiss on her lips as he moved to the desk. Her fingers delved into his hair, tangled themselves tight, the pressure making him groan as his lust urged him on.

He set her down on the desk with her legs draped over the edge. He fisted handfuls of silk, the material cold compared to the electrifying warmth of her thighs as he bared them to his touch and moved between them. His other hand wound around the back of her neck and kept her lips fused to his.

Somewhere in the back of his mind, common sense tried to break through. He almost stopped, stepped back from the precipice of desire.

And then his fingers grazed the silky skin between her thighs, damp, hot and completely naked. He froze.

"Clara."

He didn't recognize his own voice—harsh, grating, dark and heavy with a lust he'd never experienced.

She arched her hips against his touch. His fingers moved of their own accord, stroking her wet heat.

"I didn't…" Her voice trailed off as she started to pull back. Uncertainty flitted across her face. "I didn't plan for this—"

He silenced her with another kiss. It didn't matter if she hadn't worn panties to torment him or for some other reason. All that mattered here, now, was that she was *his*.

Her hips moved frantically, matching the thrust of his fingers as his thumb gently caressed her most sensitive skin. Dear God, she was so tight, so wet for him. When she shuddered, crying out into his mouth, he swallowed her moans of pleasure.

That's enough. It had to be enough. He couldn't let things go further…

Dimly, he heard the hiss of a zipper. A moment later, her fingers wrapped around his hard length and he couldn't hold back his groan. Her hand pumped up and down, a motion that nearly made him embarrass himself. He grabbed her wrist and stilled her movement.

"Condom," he ground out.

"I'm on the pill."

She started to reach for him again, her head lowering. The thought of her exquisite mouth wrapped around him nearly undid him once more.

"Next time." When she started to argue, he silenced her by kissing her mouth before trailing his lips across her cheek and along her jaw. "I need to be inside you."

Her legs spread, her body moving to the edge of the desk. He guided himself to her core, gently pressed against her, teasing both of them into a frenetic frenzy before he finally gave in to both their needs and plunged inside her welcoming body. She closed around him as if she'd been made for him. Her head dropped back, baring her neck to his lips, his tongue, his relentless need. She grabbed on to his shoulders, met him thrust for thrust as he took everything she gave and demanded more.

"Alaric… I can't… I'm so…"

He wrapped his arms around her, tangled one hand in her hair and kissed her senseless as she came apart in his arms. He followed a second later, growling into her mouth as he claimed her body and soul.

CHAPTER TWO

Five weeks later

THE TESTS WERE lined up like little toy soldiers, five in total. Each one said the same thing.

PREGNANT

Why, Clara mused as she drummed her fingers on the edge of the bathroom sink, *did they put that word in all capital letters?* Like the tests were shouting just how big a mistake she'd made.

Because she'd made a colossal one. Not only had she not planned on having a child anytime soon, if ever, but having her boss's baby catapulted the situation from *uh-oh* to catastrophic.

She turned sideways. Her stomach was still flat. She'd chalked the bone-deep exhaustion up to overseeing the royal wedding, her loss of appetite to the time of year. The anniversary of Miles's death always left her tossing all night, afraid of the nightmares waiting for her on the other side of sleep. Even though her brief marriage to the scion of Clemont Oil had been a deeply unhappy one, it didn't wipe away the guilt embedded in her bones.

Guilt that Miles's death had, at least partially, been her fault.

It's why she'd taken an herbal remedy every night the last month. It knocked her into a dreamless state that made life possible until the anniversary passed and the memories faded.

But that sleep had come at a price. After the fifth test, an online search had revealed that herbal remedy also decreased the effectiveness of the pill.

Panic fluttered in her chest. Should she wait to tell Alaric until a doctor confirmed her pregnancy? Or should she get the big reveal over with?

Alaric's handsome face appeared in her mind. Normally his dark, chiseled features were frozen in a cold mask, a permanent poker face that gave nothing away, including his innermost thoughts and desires. The first couple of years she'd worked for him, his harsh attractiveness hadn't fazed her. Her heart had been too battered and wary to entertain anything beyond acknowledgment that the prince was extremely good-looking. She knew, too, between his own hints and palace gossip, that he wasn't living like a monk in the years leading up to his wedding. Neither was his fiancée, although her indulgences had played out across the press with increasing frequency compared to the shroud of secrecy Alaric had conducted his affairs under.

Still, as she'd healed and started to regain threads of her lost confidence over the last couple of years, she'd been grateful for the rarely-spoken-of engagement. It kept her mind where it belonged: on her work and off her unattainable boss's broad shoulders, dark gaze and razor-sharp wit. Easier said than done the more he'd sought her out, talked with her and, most importantly, listened. A stark contrast from Miles's preference for her to be seen, not heard. And Alaric's passion for the country he would one day inherit added another seductive layer to the intoxicating mix that was Prince Alaric Van Ambrose.

But there had always been Miss Celestine Osborne in the background. Alaric's future wife.

Until last year. Until That Night, as she'd come to think of it. The night when the innocent little flutterings in her belly and enjoyment she received from their talks had crackled into something more intense.

The night Alaric had ceased being just a prince and shown her that he was most definitely a hot-blooded man.

The tapping of her fingers intensified as she remembered Alaric, stripped to the waist with sweat glistening on his back as he'd pummeled the punching bag in his private gym. When he'd looked at her, she'd barely stopped herself from tripping over her own two feet at the intensity in his gaze. A mix of heated anger and raw pain at complete odds with the calm, controlled prince who had dealt with both his fiancée's and his father's machinations with a disapproving yet bored air.

He hadn't let up on the bag, delivering blow after blow as he'd released all the hurt and fury that had to have been building for years. She'd felt like a voyeur, her eyes riveted to the ripples of muscle as his body had moved with lightning speed. Desire had wound its way

through her veins with an intensity she hadn't anticipated. She'd never experienced that intoxicating, languid heat, so potent she'd almost felt bewitched.

"I don't want your pity," he'd snapped at her.

Anyone else might have mistaken his growl for an
order. But she'd sensed the undercurrents running beneath his words. He didn't want her support, fine. But
the man needed someone to tell him exactly what she
had:

You just deserve better.

The tapping ceased as she grabbed the sink in a death
grip. What on earth had she been thinking, crossing
that line with him? An innocuous comment that had
taken the spark they'd both ignored and fanned it into
a slow-burning flame. A flame that had suddenly burst
out of control into an all-out blaze that had shocked her
to her very core.

Even now, despite the exhaustion that had etched
dark half-moons into the skin below her eyes, her body
tingled at the memory of how they'd melted into each
other, his fingers tangling in her hair as if to anchor her
against him, his mouth plundering, possessing, mark-
ing her with his passion.

She picked up the last test and walked into the
kitchen. As she set about preparing the teakettle, she
kept glancing at the screen, as though if enough time
passed, the answer might change and free her from
this hell.

But the word remained. The kettle whistled. She
huffed her frustration and shoved the test toward the
back of the counter near a vase of flowers before grabbing the kettle off the stove and pouring the steaming

water into a mug. She would need to deal with it at some point.

Just not now.

A knock sounded on her door and startled her out of her musings.

"Just a minute."

"Miss Stephenson, open up."

Her heart leaped into her throat as Alaric's deep voice rumbled through her. She gripped the sink and made eye contact with her pale reflection.

"Get it together. You have a royal wedding to manage."

She sucked in a deep breath, released the sink and breathed out.

Straighten your shoulders. Smooth your hair. Be professional.

With that last reminder echoing in her mind, she walked out into the spacious main room of the suite she'd called home for the last seven years.

Another knock sounded, this one brisker and louder.

"Miss Stephenson."

Irritation chased away some of her fear. Not just because Alaric was used to getting what he wanted whenever he snapped his fingers. No, she was irritated because the blasted man had slipped easily from his brief role of lover back to heir apparent and prince without batting an eye. Even the camaraderie that had materialized and grown since the Christmas dinner debacle last year had disappeared, replaced by the proper boss-and-underling relationship once more.

Whereas she had spent the past five weeks fighting to keep her eyes on his face instead of drifting lower, her traitorous mind providing vivid memories of what lay beneath his tailored suits.

The doorknob suffered her wrath as she twisted it with extra force and yanked the door open.

Did he have to look so handsome and put-together all the time? With his nearly six-and-a-half-foot height and broad shoulders, he towered over almost everyone in the palace. Emerald-green eyes pierced her from beneath thick dark brows. His face, classically handsome with carved cheekbones, a square jaw and sculpted lips, was normally set in a cold, apathetic mask.

Which made his glower ten times more alarming. Normally his imperious expressions didn't have an effect on her. It's what had made her an effective executive assistant, her ability to withstand his firm manner and short-worded orders.

"Your Highness? Is everything all right?"

Alaric's eyes traveled up and down her body, taking in her bathrobe and bare feet. She resisted the urge to pull the robe tighter. Ridiculous that she should feel vulnerable after what they'd done in his study.

Specifically on his desk, her skirt around her waist, his masterful hands on her thighs as he'd teased her most vulnerable skin with gentle, fleeting strokes before he'd thrust—

"I didn't realize robes were acceptable wedding attire."

His pompous tone threw cold water on her heated remembering.

"It's seven thirty in the morning. The wedding starts at five." She released her death grip on her robe and casually put one hand on the door frame, filling up the doorway in a manner meant to keep him in the hallway and out of her private sanctuary. "Didn't you read the schedule I emailed yesterday?"

He lifted a brow. "I did. Isn't the florist arriving at eight?"

Oh, no. It took significant effort to keep her expression neutral.

"Meira is showing them into the ballroom."

Both eyebrows climbed up. "Since when do you let your assistant do anything without you hovering?"

"I trained her. And she's a friend. Of course I trust her."

He leaned down. The scent of pine teased her, woodsy and crisp, like walking through a forest draped in snow.

"Since when?"

Her frown deepened. "What's this really about, Your Highness?"

"What?"

"Why are you here, at my private apartment, the morning of your sister's wedding, asking about how I've organized the day when I've kept this palace running for seven years?"

Something flickered in the chilly, sharp depths of his eyes. But then he blinked and it disappeared as he straightened.

"Ensuring my sister's wedding day is going smoothly doesn't sound like an unreasonable request to me."

She bit back a sigh. No, it wasn't unreasonable. She had picked a horrible day to go off script and not be ready to go her customary thirty minutes ahead of schedule.

Plus, if she kept fighting him, he might start asking

more questions. What if she didn't have an answer or, worse, what if she became flustered and blurted out something she shouldn't?

"I apologize, Your Highness. I just need to get dressed. I'll be in the grand ballroom in ten minutes."

She started to close the door, but Alaric put a hand up to stop her.

"I didn't come up here to chastise you."

The thinnest thread of apology in his voice nearly undid her. Exhaustion sank into her skin, penetrated her bones in one fell swoop.

"Whatever your reasons, Your Highness, you are entitled to them." *Now would you just go away?* "If you'll excuse me, I really must get dressed."

She must be more tired than she initially realized. Because as she started to turn away, she could have sworn she saw frustration tighten his mouth and darken his eyes. Alaric Van Ambrose didn't get frustrated. He didn't get excited. He didn't get anything. He was aloof, detached, unemotional.

Sometimes she wondered if she'd even imagined that night in the gym, read too much into what she had perceived as the more relaxed nature of their working relationship the past year. If it wasn't for the very physical proof of their lovemaking, she probably could have convinced herself that she'd dreamed about the burning heat of his gaze, the simmering passion that had boiled over as their bodies had joined in a frantic dance of need and pent-up desire.

"Clara."

It took her a moment to realize he'd said it out loud, the first time he'd used it since he'd growled it right before his lips had slanted over hers, sent a shock of electricity through her veins. She jumped, started to turn. A hand fell on her shoulder, pressed the fluffy material flush against her skin. She jerked away, her breath coming out in a sharp exhale.

"Clara!"

Hands closed over her arms, steadied her. She sucked in a deep breath. Her lungs filled with his scent, the woodsy smell calming the rapid beating of her heart.

"Clara, if you don't speak now, I'm calling the doctor and—"

"I'm fine, Your Highness." She blinked rapidly and her vision filled with him: strong jaw tight with worry, full lips stretched into a thin line, the fit of his black pants and navy sweater on his muscular build.

"You're not fine."

"Look, I didn't sleep well, and I'm just feeling a little under the weather." She stepped back but he didn't relinquish his grip on her arms.

"You're pale, you have bags under your eyes, and you just jumped out of your skin. 'Under the weather' is an understatement."

This time she managed to wrench free of his hold and took a large, purposeful step back.

"Just the words a girl needs to hear when she's sick."

Sick. Pregnant with your illegitimate child.

"I'm sending for the doctor." Alaric turned away. "You're right. Meira can handle the initial setup until you're cleared."

She stood there, mouth agape, as he disappeared from view. Then common sense returned and she rushed to the door.

"Your Highness, I—"

"That's an order, Miss Stephenson." The haughty jerk didn't even bother looking over his shoulder as he stalked down the hall. "One you'll follow if you want to keep your job."

CHAPTER THREE

ALARIC'S EYES ROAMED the ballroom. Somewhere among the designer dresses and tailored tuxedos, a pale-haired woman in a blue dress glided through the crowds and elegantly set tables. A stubborn woman with blue eyes that could cut a man down to size one second and make him drop to his knees the next with a seductive need that burned in his veins long after she'd left.

Christ, get a grip.

He was at his sister's wedding. His little sister's wedding, for God's sake.

White lilies and red hydrangeas bloomed from glass vases. Candles flickered on crimson tablecloths, creating an intimate environment in the massive grand ballroom hosting Prince Cassius and Princess Briony Adama's wedding reception. Chandeliers sparkled overhead, with scarlet roses placed strategically among the glittering strands. White-gloved waiters cleared china, refilled champagne glasses and passed out trays of chocolate-covered eclairs, slices of tarte aux pommes topped with sliced apples and melted apricot jam, and macarons.

Judging by the beaming smile on Briony's face as

Cass swept her onto the dance floor, she was having the time of her life. Everything was perfect. It always was when Clara was involved.

So why, Alaric asked himself for the twentieth time that day, had he come down so hard on Clara that morning?

Because you can't stop thinking about her. Ever since their tryst in his office last month, he'd been disgusted with himself. Disgust that he had not only abandoned his scruples and had sex with an employee, but that he had done so in such a coarse manner.

Just like your father.

He swallowed a larger amount of gin than he'd intended, focused on the burn of the citrusy liquid. He would have to confront his actions, and his fears, at some point. Especially the intensity of his attraction to his secretary.

Executive assistant.

He frowned into his glass. His engagement to Celestine Osborne may have lasted for almost a decade, but he'd had no emotional connection to his betrothed. How could he when he'd only seen her a handful of times since their engagement officially started? Her telling him at that first meeting that she would be living her life as if she were single up until their wedding had certainly not made him inclined to entertain romantic thoughts, either. He hadn't blamed her; she had been just shy of twenty when her father had pledged her hand in marriage to Alaric.

When Celestine had told him her intentions, he'd been only too happy to follow her lead. For the next several years, he had conducted a couple of discreet affairs with women who knew marriage was off the table. They'd been pleasant, mutually beneficial and pleasurable relationships that had sustained him as he'd taken a more active role in Linnaea's government. A necessary move given how little his father, King Daxon Van Ambrose, bothered to involve himself in anything but spending the treasury's money. A habit that had been the driving force behind the Van Ambrose-Osborne marriage contract.

Except that insidious fear had crept in once more.

Am I like my father?

At first it had just been an adolescent worry. But it had started to rear its head as the people of Linnaea had started to look to him more, as his duties became clearer. He'd terminated his romantic liaisons two years ago not just because the deadline for his marriage to Celestine was drawing nearer, but because his fear had started to overshadow every encounter with another woman who wasn't his fiancée, no matter how atrocious her behavior or outrageous her antics. He'd made excuses long enough, but in the end, he was enjoying the company and beds of women he wasn't pledged to.

Just like Daxon.

No matter that Celestine had apparently more than outmatched him in the number of bedmates, and done so as publicly as possible. Unlike his mother, too, who had loved his wastrel of a father until her dying day, Celestine hadn't felt anything close to love for him. Those facts hadn't made a dent in the guilt that had dug into his veins.

Alaric loathed any hint of scandal. He could still

remember hearing his mother's sobs through the hotel room door on a trip to London when he'd been all of four years old and his father had left a dinner with the wife of a Foreign Office official. It was the first vivid memory he had of the damage Daxon wrought with his selfishness, although he had plenty of moments to pick from since then. From using the illegitimate daughter he'd never met as a bargaining piece in yet another marriage contract to spending money on vanity projects like an art museum and a high-rise, Daxon seemed determined to outdo himself time and again.

Alaric made himself reach for a glass of water and take a long drink before indulging in another sip of gin. Reminiscing about the past, especially when it involved his father, made the idea of taking the edge off with a drink all too appealing. Daxon, thankfully, had excused himself at the beginning of the reception. Still licking his wounds, no doubt.

Oddly enough, Alaric's romantic interlude with Clara, coupled with the loss of the Osborne money, had propelled him to do what he should have done a long time ago: strip Daxon of his power. The members of Parliament, who could have best been described as window dressing until a month ago, had been all too happy to unite with Alaric and offer Daxon the choice of retaining his title of king but stepping down from any actual position of power and living out the remainder of his life with a small allowance and the few shreds of his dignity intact, or face a very public inquiry into his spending.

His lips tilted up as he remembered Daxon's shocked

expression when Alaric had given him his two options. He'd granted the old devil the gift of sharing the news in the privacy of his office, even if a vindictive part had longed for a public outing in front of Parliament and the various committees who had worked so hard with Alaric to keep the country running the last few years. Daxon had blustered, argued, yelled and, for one horrifying minute, blubbered.

But the threat of censure, of finally having to face his decades of mistakes, had been enough. He'd stepped down from the public eye, citing his cancer diagnosis, and turned over Linnaea's government to Alaric and Parliament. The shackles that had kept Alaric's hands tied, loosened by Celestine breaking their engagement, had fallen away. Though it wouldn't have been possible without the money brought in by Briony's marriage to Cass and the new agreement with Switzerland.

Best not to look that gift horse in the mouth. The timing had been perfect. He, and Linnaea, were free to move forward.

Amazing the number of changes that had occurred since his engagement from hell had ended.

A flash of pale gold hair caught his eye among the sea of designer dresses, tailored tuxedos and overpriced jewelry. His eyes narrowed as he watched Clara dart about, checking in with vendors and making notes on her tablet.

The dratted woman had openly defied him that morning. When he'd returned to her apartment with the palace's physician, she hadn't answered. When he'd let himself in, worried she might have passed out, it was to find an empty suite of rooms. She'd ignored his calls, responded to his texts with as few words as possible and skillfully avoided him all day.

Why?

The second question that had been bugging him all day. The last five weeks Clara had been nothing but professional. She ran his schedule with the same ruthless efficiency she'd displayed the last seven years. She'd attended all of her meetings, addressed him formally and…

And acted as if she hadn't arched her body against his, her fingers tangled in his hair, his lips pressed in a heated kiss against the pulse pounding in her neck as he drove deep inside her.

Blood rushed through his veins as her husky moans and frantic murmuring of his name echoed in his mind. Thank God he was sitting down so the evidence of his lurid musings wasn't observed by his sister's wedding guests.

Had they not had wild sex in his office, he wouldn't have gone up to her room this morning. That had been a mistake. But then again, so had allowing her to slip under his skin over the last year, to pay attention to the subtle nuances of her character like the flash in her eyes when she got frustrated or the sharp wit in her texts and emails. Those indulgences, letting his guard down and treating her more as a partner than an employee, had ripped away his self-control in the moment when he'd needed it most.

His eyes found, then clung to her svelte form clad in navy blue. She moved through the crowd, confidence evident in the set of her shoulders, the lift of her chin.

What was it about her? Had the stress of last year's dinner made him latch onto the nearest woman who conducted herself with decorum? Had the unexpected breakup led to what could be chalked up as a simple bad decision?

Or was his worst fear true? That he'd inherited his father's uncontrollable desires? He'd spent years working to distance himself from King Daxon Van Ambrose and his legacy of selfishness and greed.

But perhaps he was more like his sire than he knew.

Coldness crept in and chased away the lingering warmth from the gin. If the last was true, and he had surrendered to nothing more than lust, he and Clara would have to evaluate whether reassigning her to another role in the palace would be in both their interests.

He didn't care for that thought. But being the heir didn't mean he always got his way. It usually meant the exact opposite.

Briony swept up to him, her smile more radiant than her gold wedding gown.

"Why are you over here by yourself?" she asked as she sat in a swirl of tulle and satin.

"I'm not the star of the show. I'm enjoying a rare moment of solitude."

Briony rolled her eyes. "Rare? You go out of your way to avoid people."

"Only ones I don't like."

"You don't like anyone."

His eyes drifted to where he had last seen Clara. When he glanced back at his sister, it was to see a suspiciously satisfied smirk on her face.

"What?"

"Nothing."

A childish urge to tweak a stray red curl made him

clasp his hands around his gin glass. As much as he had come to care for his half sister, there were times having a younger sibling made him grit his teeth.

"Are you enjoying your wedding ball?"

The teasing glint disappeared as her green eyes, so like his own, lit up.

"It's magical," she breathed as she gazed around the candlelit ballroom. "It's hard to believe two months ago I was slinging drinks in Kansas."

"And that a prince would sweep you off your feet."

"That, too," Briony agreed with a light laugh.

Prince Cassius Adama, Alaric's new brother-in-law, appeared at her side and leaned down to press a kiss to his new wife's forehead. Alaric had despised Cass when the man had appeared out of nowhere and essentially blackmailed Daxon into letting him marry Briony. But surprisingly, not only had the two fallen in love, but Cass was genuinely invested in helping Linnaea reclaim financial independence.

Alaric nodded to Cass. He liked to think that confronting Cass the morning after he'd broken off his engagement with Briony had had something to do with the couple reuniting.

Cass returned the nod before glancing around. "Didn't mean to interrupt, but has anyone checked on Clara?"

Unease made Alaric frown. "Checked on her?"

"I just saw her leaving the ballroom. She looked paler than usual."

Alaric was on his feet and moving before either of the newlyweds could utter another word. What was the little fool trying to do? Kill herself with work? He'd always admired Clara's strength, work ethic. But she'd never been this stubborn before.

A mining heiress, several dignitaries and an American pop star interrupted his journey. He forced himself to accept their well wishes, frustration seething beneath his normally calm exterior.

At last, he extracted himself and reached the main hallway outside the ballroom. Some partygoers were clustered off to the right. To the left was an empty hall, save for the lone guard heading off any inquisitive guests who might want to access the royal family's private quarters.

"Cecil."

"Your Highness," the guard replied as he snapped to attention.

"Did Miss Stephenson come this way?"

"Yes, Your Highness. Less than five minutes ago."

"How was she?"

Cecil paused for the briefest of moments. He was new to the guard, barely out of university. Judging by the indecision on his face, Clara had warned him not to say anything.

"Cecil, I'm asking you as your future king."

"Yes, Your Highness. She looked ill. Said she was feeling faint."

Alaric swore softly.

"Thank you, Cecil."

He strode past the guard, turned right and headed for the elevator.

Until a glimpse of blond hair caught his eye. He stopped, keeping his face smooth even as his pulse started to pound at the sight of Clara sitting on a bench tucked into an alcove, her skin too pale, her chest rising and falling with her rapid breathing.

"Clara?"

Her eyes flew open, the blue even more vivid against the pallor of her skin.

"I just need to rest."

"You need a hospital," he ground out as he strode forward and knelt at her side.

"No, I don't," she retorted, her voice surprisingly strong. "And if you try to pick me up and carry me out to an ambulance, I will scream."

Despite the worry coursing through his body, his lips twitched.

"What if I gave you an order as your future king?"

"I'm a British national. You're my boss, not my king."

Her face contorted and one hand flew to her mouth.

"I just need to lie down. I'm feeling a little sick to my stomach."

"Nausea?" he repeated. Something flickered in the back of his mind, a notion he couldn't quite grasp.

"Something I ate."

Her gaze skittered to the side. His eyes narrowed. Before he could press her, she pushed off the bench and teetered. He stood and wrapped an arm around her slender waist.

"Go back to the reception," she protested as she pushed at his arm.

"No. I'm making sure you get back to your apartment without passing out."

Her lips parted to argue.

"Nonnegotiable, Miss Stephenson." Blue fire flashed

in her eyes as her mouth thinned into a straight line. But she didn't argue as he guided her to the elevator.

Worry and unwanted awareness thickened the air in the elevator. The palm of his hand, splayed cross the curve of her hip, grew warm as the heat of her skin seeped through the thin material of her gown.

Disgust tightened his throat as his body reacted. The one time he'd confronted his father about his affairs and the toll they'd taken on Queen Marianne, a month before his mother passed, Daxon had said he just couldn't help himself when he saw a pretty woman.

And now here he was, the faint scent of roses making his heartbeat quicken, as Clara grew paler by the moment.

Pervert. Selfish jerk. Bastard.

The words he'd leveled at his father before he'd stalked out of the room pounded through his head, each damning word making him want to revisit his gym and punch the bag until he collapsed from exhaustion.

He slowly loosened his hold on her waist and, once he was sure Clara wasn't going to topple over, released her completely. He needed to reassign her. Immediately. This wasn't her fault. No, it was his. His for letting himself lose control too many times, for not having enough strength to resist his own chaotic desires.

Clara deserved better.

When they reached her room on the top floor of the castle, she paused outside her door.

"Thank you, Your Highness."

"I will leave once I know you're safe."

The door swung open. Clara walked in, her shoulders tense as she moved into her apartment. He didn't bother to disguise his curiosity as he looked around, making sure to keep plenty of physical distance between the two of them even as he kept an eagle eye on her form should she suddenly start to collapse. When he'd been in there earlier, he'd been so focused on finding her, and then so incensed by her outright defiance, he hadn't bothered to take note of her residence. With Clara's toned-down style and ruthless efficiency, he'd expect a minimalist approach, lots of clean lines and white and black. Not the pale blue walls, dove-gray sofa scattered with colorful pillows or twinkling lights draped over the fireplace mantel.

His eyes drifted to Clara as she kicked off her heels and sank into an overstuffed chair by the fireplace. What else did he not know about his assistant of seven years and onetime lover?

Drop it.

Common sense chased away his curiosity. The more he wondered, the more he blurred the lines between work and his personal life, the more he courted trouble.

Taking her on your desk didn't count as blurring the lines? a voice taunted in his ear.

Clara's shuddering breath broke through his thoughts.

"Thank you again, Your Highness."

He gritted his teeth. The formal address was appropriate and a reminder of their stations. It shouldn't bother him. Just another example that she was behaving professionally.

While he was remembering how incredible her body had felt beneath his hands.

"You're welcome." A quick glance at her face confirmed that she was still too pale. "I'm going to get you a glass of water before I leave."

She started to stand.

"I can get it—"

"Sit," he ordered as he crossed the room.

That she only shot him a minimal glare before sinking back down into the depths of the chair let him know just how exhausted she felt.

He walked into the kitchen and pulled a glass out of a cabinet. He kept his gaze focused on the water flowing from the faucet, not on the little details begging for his attention: the photos on the refrigerator that hinted at a life outside of the palace, a vase of flowers in the corner, a book lying facedown on the counter.

As he turned off the faucet, something caught his attention—a little white stick sitting next to the vase.

A dull roaring built in his ears. The apartment faded as his vision narrowed. He reached out, pulled the stick closer and read the single word still visible on the screen.

His fingers tightened around the test as white-hot anger stormed past the walls of his usual restraint. How long had she known? How long had she concealed the truth from him? Clara had always struck him as honest and honorable. Yet she had hidden something that literally changed not just the course of both their lives, but the future of the country.

He breathed in, then out, tamping down the fires of his fury to simmering embers that he could control. Then, slowly, he turned and walked back to the mother of his child, keeping the test partially concealed in his hand.

He handed her the water, watched her drink it. She murmured a thank-you, handed him back the glass, then frowned as he pressed the test into her hand. He hadn't thought it possible for her face to turn any paler, but any color she'd regained disappeared as her eyes widened before flying up to meet his gaze.

His face settled into what Clara had once called his "ice mask." Frozen, she'd said, like his features had been carved from granite by the devil.

"You lied to me. So," he said as he sat down on the ottoman in front of the chair and put his hands on the armrests, caging her in, "we need to make some decisions, Miss Stephenson."

She swallowed hard but didn't look away. He despised the flicker of admiration in his chest. She didn't deserve anything right now but his anger.

"Like what?" she finally asked.

He smiled, the gesture anything but pleasant.

"Like when we should get married."

CHAPTER FOUR

CLARA STARED AT ALARIC.

Did he just say "married"?

"What?"

"Married."

Yes, he did.

She blinked a couple of times, her brain grasping for a response. It finally settled on, "Why?"

His icy smile disappeared, replaced by a quelling glance that all but shouted how foolish she was for not immediately realizing where he was going with this.

"You're carrying the heir to the Linnaean throne."

Her eyes drifted back down to the test. Over twelve hours had passed since her suspicions had been confirmed, and it still didn't seem real. She'd caught herself glancing at her reflection more than once as she'd moved throughout the day. But no matter how many times she'd looked, her belly had remained flat, her body showing no outward signs that a child was growing inside her.

"And?"

Alaric's muscles tightened, the material of his suit sleeves stretching across his biceps.

"And I will be damned before I allow my child to be born out of wedlock and see his or her legacy tainted by scandal."

The words whipped out and slashed at her with the viciousness of a dagger. She barely kept her expression smooth. Alaric knew of her former marriage, was aware that her husband had perished in a car accident. But aside from her former in-laws, who had no desire to see the truth come to light, the details of her horrendous marriage and that horrific night had died with Miles.

Still, that word never failed to make her inwardly flinch.

Scandal.

Her mother-in-law had screeched it at Clara in the bedroom adjoining Miles's master suite in his luxury penthouse, full of expensive paintings and sculptures that didn't go with anything but had signaled loudly to all visitors that someone with money and culture resided there. Temperance Clemont had looked the opposite of cultured as she'd threatened Clara with lawsuits, jail and other horrific consequences, including "a scandal she'd never live down," for not saving her son.

Temperance had at least been partially right. Clara had done what she'd done too many times with Miles—let her own fears stop her from doing the right thing. In this case, stop Miles from getting behind the wheel after he'd had so much to drink he'd barely been able to stand up.

But Temperance's accusations, that Clara had somehow orchestrated the event to get to Miles's money… that had been going too far. It had only been because she managed to snag a copy of the police report, the one proving that Miles had been drunk, before Temperance had had it buried that she had any leverage against her mother-in-law and her oil baron husband, Stanley. After she'd returned Temperance's threats with some of her own, they'd slipped away to one of their oceanside mansions and left her finally, blissfully alone.

Except for the sick feeling that developed in the pit of her stomach whenever she heard that word. That it was being flung at her by the father of her child made it ten times worse.

"Marriage is not the answer."

Alaric blinked. Had she surprised him? The possibility that he had expected her to thank him and quickly agree to turn her life, and that of the baby's, over to him chased away her nausea.

"It is the only answer, Clara."

Anger pulsed through her veins and gave her enough strength to sit up straight, bringing her within inches of Alaric. Miles had pressured her into getting engaged long before she was ready, and damn it, she'd let him. She'd been so lost after losing her mother, just a few years after losing her father, and had let her craving for a family override her gut feeling that her relationship with Miles had moved far too quickly, that while he was fun to be around he was not husband material. That one concession had led to another, then one more, until suddenly she'd had nothing left of herself but her name.

The penthouse, with its rooftop garden and indoor swimming pool, had quickly revealed itself for what it was beneath the glitter and expensive furnishings: a gilded cage. It had started out slowly, with Miles encouraging her to stay home and enjoy newlywed life, before progressing into ordering her to tell him her every movement when she left. His controlling demands had taken their toll to the point that she'd stopped going out unless he told her to accompany him somewhere. Easier to wither away in the penthouse than risk a furious tantrum from her husband.

The first time she'd left the house after his death, she'd paused so long in the lobby the doorman had approached to ask if she was all right. Stepping out into the blistering wind of a London winter had been so refreshing she hadn't been able to hold back her smile or the tears of relief that had followed.

Nothing, including a prince used to getting his way, would make her give up her independence again.

"Not for me."

"Because you've been married once before?"

"Yes. Once was enough."

His eyes swept over her face, assessing, probing, delving deeper than anyone, including Miles, ever had. She didn't flinch, didn't pull away as one hand drifted up to rest against her cheek. He'd touched her in far more intimate places a month ago.

"Why?"

"My husband was spoiled and self-centered," she replied matter-of-factly. "The man I dated was not the man I married. Marriage was not enjoyable. I don't see myself repeating the experience."

Alaric's face softened as she spoke, something almost akin to compassion lighting his emerald gaze. But the brief empathy disappeared at her refusal.

"Yes. You will."

She stood, her quick movement making his hand

fall away and forcing him to move back. Was it wrong to take pleasure in knowing she'd literally thrown him off-balance? *Probably*, she thought as she walked to her door and held it open, *but I'm too tired to care*.

"No, I won't. I'm sick. You have a wedding reception to be at. I have no desire to keep you from being involved if you want to be, but I'm not marrying you." Pride at her ability to stand up for herself straightened her spine and strengthened her voice. "We'll discuss options in the morning."

Alaric drew himself up to his very imposing height. Broad shoulders that reminded her of the mountains beyond the palace that stretched up to the sky, tall, daunting and magnificent. Her body stirred as he stalked toward her, each step slow and deliberate, muscles rippling beneath the fine cloth of his suit.

When he'd held her in his arms, cradled her body against him as though she'd been crafted from spun glass as they'd both drifted down from the incredible peak of passion, she'd nearly wept. Wept from the sheer pleasure, wept from how incredibly alive she'd felt...

And wept because, for one moment, she'd felt cherished. Cared for.

Dangerous emotions that could lead down a fatal path, as she'd learned all too well. The difference was that, when Miles had showered her with gifts and compliments, she'd been starved for affection, left adrift by her parents' death and feeling isolated among the bustling streets of London, a far cry from the small town she'd been raised in. He'd picked up a book she'd dropped outside the lecture hall at the University of London, shooting her a thousand-watt smile that had seemed like sunshine cutting through the cloud of grief she'd been under since her mother's death the year before. He'd insisted on walking her to class, then taking her out to dinner, which had ended up being a private dinner cruise on the Thames. She knew now that her responses, overflowing with gratitude and praise, had fed into Miles's ego. They'd created a vicious cycle for themselves that had whirled them through their courtship so quickly she hadn't paid attention to the steadily growing warning signs until it was too late.

Now, no matter how incredible Alaric had made her feel, no matter how much she enjoyed his company, she knew that she didn't need it to survive. And she certainly didn't want it when the so-called proposal was rooted in necessity and, judging by the harsh set of Alaric's jaw, anger.

Guilt punched through her own frustration. Alaric had suggested more protection. But after she'd mentioned being on the pill—*stupid*—they had both given in to the heat of the moment and eschewed any rational thought in favor of surrendering to lust.

She lifted her chin in the air as he stopped in front of her, staring down at her with hard eyes, quiet wrath radiating off his body.

"I am the heir apparent. 'No' is not an answer I'm used to hearing."

Was it wrong to feel disappointed in his reply? His world had been turned upside down in the last two months, from a long-lost sister and sudden royal marriage to his own engagement being broken and now a child on the way.

Still, the Alaric she knew wouldn't reply like a

spoiled brat not getting his way, not when it was just the two of them. What if the man she thought she'd gotten to know, the man she'd felt closer to than anyone over the past few months, was just like Miles—an image she'd built up in her head?

"Then perhaps you need to hear it more often." She gestured to the open door. "Because that's all you'll get from me. I won't keep the baby from you. But I am not marrying you."

He stepped closer. She breathed in and was hit by a familiar scent: pine and spice, a sensual, masculine mix that had wound itself into her psyche since that night in the gym. Except now, after being surrounded by that fragrance as Alaric had placed an open-mouthed kiss to the pulse frantically beating in her throat, his tongue dancing over her skin with an expertise that had set fire to her as he'd moved inside her body, it was no longer just a casual aroma. It ignited her senses, stirred memories better left in the past and, worst of all, lowered her defenses.

What would it be like, she wondered for the span of a heartbeat, to say yes? To be married to a man she respected, who always acted in the best interests of his country and the throne? Who had shown her a side of passion she'd never imagined could exist?

Her hand drifted toward her stomach before she caught herself. What would it be like to have a father in her child's life? Something she herself had been so fortunate to have and had missed so terribly when cancer had cruelly snatched him away?

But what if she would be married to a man who, like her former husband, wanted what he wanted when he wanted it?

No, thanks.

He leaned down, his lips stopping a breath away from hers. For a moment she was seized with a mad desire to raise up on her toes and kiss him. Would it shock him? Would she experience satisfaction that she had thrown him off-balance again in less than a minute?

Or would he do what Alaric did best: take control?

Worry flickered through her. When it came to anything regarding his beloved Linnaea, Alaric had no problem sacrificing any personal gains if it meant a better outcome for the country. He'd dethroned his own father. What sort of definitive action would he take regarding her and their child?

"I have no desire to see this become a legal issue."

His voice trailed off, leaving a wealth of meaning lingering on the air as the hairs on her arms stood straight up.

"Don't threaten me, Alaric Van Ambrose."

"It's not a threat, Clara. It's a fact, the only route available if you decline my offer of marriage." Pity softened his gaze. She hated it. "It's not how I want things to proceed. But you of all people must understand why it's imperative that we marry and this child is not only protected but has a clear path to the throne."

Deep inside, the part of her that had fallen in love with Linnaea, that had adopted the country as her own and fought tooth and nail alongside Alaric the past seven years to free it from Daxon's selfish ruling, understood all too well.

But the thought of being pressured into another marriage made her feel as if she was being slowly but steadily pushed into a tiny room, one where the walls closed in until she could barely breathe.

Trapped until the day she died.

She started as Alaric's hand settled on her arm, firm and warm. Comforting. It shouldn't be. She should resist it all costs. She'd let Miles entice her into marriage against her better judgment. How she could be such a fool to let herself repeat the mistakes of the past?

"We'll meet at ten a.m. in my office." His voice was infinitely gentler, coaxing. It lured her in, made her want to believe that things could be as easy as saying yes. More hazardous to her heart than Miles ever had been. Even in her grief, some part of her had been aware that Miles's charm had only existed on the surface. She'd just told herself that it would get better with time, so desperate had she been to move past the grief of losing her mother and being alone in the world with no family of her own.

Stupid, stupid, stupid.

The qualities she liked about Alaric, his leadership, his integrity, his steadfast commitment to duty, were embedded in his character and as real as the child growing inside her. Even if the burgeoning intimacy between them was an illusion she'd created, she didn't doubt the abilities that had first stoked her admiration and, eventually, the crush that had developed. He was everything Miles hadn't been. Which made him infinitely more tempting, and twice as dangerous.

It wouldn't be hard at all to fall for Alaric Van Ambrose.

She started to rebut his offer of a morning meeting,

but then conceded with a nod. Better to pick her battles, especially when she was facing down an all-out war.

"Ten a.m. Good night, Your Highness."

As soon as the door closed and she heard his footsteps recede down the hallway, her body drooped, her hand clutching the doorknob like it was a lifeline. She forced herself to breathe and summoned enough strength to wobble back to her bedroom. The thick comforter welcomed her with a pillowy embrace. Her eyes started to drift shut.

You have just a little over twelve hours to put a plan together, the rational side of her brain reminded her.

She would…after a little nap.

CHAPTER FIVE

THE DETERMINED KNOCK sounded at ten o'clock precisely. Despite his inner turmoil, a smile tugged at Alaric's lips. Clara was renowned for never arriving early or late, but precisely on time. It was why he had been so concerned by her tardiness yesterday.

The smile disappeared as he crossed the room with a determined stride. He respected that Clara was the one pregnant with their child. But it didn't stop the pride that filled his chest at the thought of finally having a child of his own to continue the legacy of the Linnaean throne. He'd barely been able to stomach the thought of touching Celestine, let alone creating children with her. Having a woman like Clara, one who was just as passionate about his country as he was, who exhibited qualities like determination, dedication and decorum, carry his child filled him with an emotion he had rarely experienced: happiness.

While he would have certainly changed the way their child's conception occurred, he couldn't regret the result. Not when he compared it to the alternative of being shackled to Celestine. Now the only thing standing in his way of achieving everything he'd worked so hard to build, including a proper royal marriage, was Clara's stubbornness.

He had never not achieved something he'd set his sights on before. He wasn't about to start losing now.

He opened the door. Clara looked up and blinked in surprise. He took advantage of her surprise to rake her with a swift gaze. She was still a touch too pale, a faint bruising beneath her eyes as if she hadn't gotten much sleep. But today, instead of glancing at her and then immediately focusing on his work, he noted the blue of her eyes, the contrast of her elfin face with the determined jut of her chin.

His mind drifted to his ex-fiancée. With coal-black hair, caramel-colored eyes and cheekbones that would have made Michelangelo weep, she'd landed on the covers of numerous magazines, lauded as one of the most beautiful women in the world despite her selfish nature and endless partying. He'd agreed with the critics, acknowledging her as physically stunning the same way he would admire a rare artifact. Only her beauty hadn't had a visceral effect on him.

The opposite of the unexpected awareness that had lodged its hooks into his skin the moment Clara had walked into that gym last Christmas. The awareness that had steadily grown, tunneling far deeper than he'd realized with the passing months, growing and morphing into a physical attraction that had exploded that night in his office. An attraction that even now burned as he looked at the mother of his child. The woman who, sooner rather than later, would be wearing his ring on her finger.

"Were you expecting someone else?" he asked drily.

"No. You usually say 'enter' instead of opening the door yourself."

"Things have changed."

A frown flickered across her face before she walked into the room and moved to her usual spot in the chair in front of his desk. She sat with the grace and aplomb of a queen.

Which was good, Alaric reflected as he followed her. Because he intended her to make her one.

"How are you feeling?"

"Better, thank you."

He sat in his chair, his eyes inadvertently drifting down to her belly.

"You're five weeks along?"

Something flashed in her eyes.

"Yes."

"And there is no other possibility?"

He kept his voice neutral, irritated at the relief that relaxed his muscles at the brief shake of her head.

"I'm assuming you could make a case against the birth control company."

A delicate pink stained her cheek.

"I… I was taking a sleep aid at the time. I didn't realize it could reduce the efficacy of the pill." She glanced down at her hands. "I'm sorry, Alaric. Truly."

When she looked back up, he nodded his acceptance of her explanation. Had it been any one of his former lovers, he would have suspected sabotage. But Clara hadn't tried to seduce him, hadn't tried to ingratiate herself in any way prior to their lovemaking. She was honest and forthright. More qualities that made her right for what he had in mind.

"So…eight months."

"Yes."

"A summer child."

"Yes."

"Will you marry me?"

One corner of her lips quirked. "No."

Admiration warred with irritation. Why did he have to break his celibacy streak with the one woman who would resist marrying a future king? His jaw tightened as his resolve strengthened. He hadn't pushed Celestine to the altar for a multitude of reasons, including his own guilt that he had essentially purchased a bride.

But this was different. The future of his child was at stake. He would go to hell and back to ensure that his son or daughter would be born with his name, his protection and the legacy of the Linnaean throne instead of the years of shame he'd suffered or the struggles Briony had grown up with.

His fingers curled into fists. Briony had claimed that her childhood was pleasant, at least until her mother had remarried, but money and security had been scarce. They'd fought for every little pleasure. Briony had struggled for months to pay for her mother's medical bills, working herself to the bone. Another result of Daxon's carelessness. He'd seduced Briony's mother, a college student studying abroad, without a care for the potential consequences.

The thought of Clara working long hours while living in some tiny ramshackle house while he resided in luxury in the royal palace made him sick to his stomach. He would not allow Clara or his child to go through a similar torture.

And it wasn't just his child's future at stake, either. It was Linnaea's future. He finally had the opportunity to chart a new course for the country, one that included a legitimate heir and a wife who would represent the country far better than her predecessor. More than once he'd wondered how Celestine would raise any children they had together. Part of him had hoped that she would continue her self-absorbed existence and leave their children to him. But that wouldn't have been ideal for their children, as he well knew, to have one parent who loved and guided them while the other barely acknowledged their presence. Once Briony had joined the royal household, he'd even toyed with the idea of not having children, of asking his sister and her husband to carry on the throne.

A frown creased his brow as he regarded Clara with a hooded gaze. She had always been an advocate for Linnaea. Perhaps she didn't understand the ramifications of what was at stake. It was no longer her decision to make, or his.

The urge to assume the mantle of Prince Alaric Van Ambrose loomed. But judging by the tense set of Clara's slender shoulders and her perch on the edge of the chair, going in guns blazing would only make her dig her heels in more. Better to start slow and make his case.

"Tell me about your first husband."

There. A blink, followed by the slightest tensing of her hands on the armrests. Whatever had happened between the Clemonts and Clara had left a mark. Judging by the tension now rolling off her slender frame, it had not been an entirely pleasant experience. He'd done quite a bit of reading on the late Miles Clemont, son of oil tycoon Stanley and former model Temperance Clemont, last night. Partly out of curiosity as to what kind of man would entice Clara Stephenson to wear his ring, but also research to arm himself for the unexpected battle she'd presented him with. She'd alluded to unhappiness in the marriage. Yet neither he nor his security firm that performed meticulous background checks had uncovered anything that would suggest what had occurred to give Clara such a negative view of matrimony.

By all accounts, the family had it all: wealth, prestige, good looks. Reviewing the numerous photos of Miles available online, mostly magazines and the occasional news feature on the work he had done with his father's company, it had been hard to picture him and Clara together. With a blindingly white smile against a deep tan and auburn hair combed back into a slick coif, Miles had oozed confidence and money.

What had Clara seen in him?

"His name was Miles Clemont. He was a consultant for Clemont Oil." She tilted her head to one side. "But you knew that already."

"We do extensive background checks on all of our hires."

"Then you know everything."

Her voice hitched up the tiniest fraction on the last word. No, he most definitely did not know anything.

"His death must have been hard on you."

"Yes."

Flat, emotionless. Anyone who took her at face value would have thought her cold and unfeeling. Most would have missed the rapid blink, the uptick of the pulse beating at the base of her throat. No, Clara was anything but impassive regarding her late husband.

"You were married for only a few months, correct?"

She looked away. "Yes. What does this have to do with our situation?"

"I'm trying to discern the reason for your refusal to see sense."

Her head whipped back around, her lips thinning as her eyes narrowed.

"See sense? Agree to marry my boss because of a one-night stand?"

His anger flared again. Anger at Clara for her ability to view their brief intimacy with detachment. Anger at her for resisting what should have been a cut-and-dried decision.

And anger at himself for letting one moment of weakness lead to this whole damn mess.

"A one-night stand that resulted in a child, Clara."

She ran a hand over her hair, dislodging the normally perfectly arranged coif so that a few strands of pale blond hair fell and framed her face.

"Women raise children on their own all the time."

"They do. But not children who will inherit the throne of Linnaea."

Her hand drifted down and settled over her stomach. Possessiveness filled his veins and nearly propelled him across the room to her side. He would protect Clara and their child. He might have made a mistake that night in his office. But he would be damned if he made any more that placed Clara in the position his father had placed women in.

"Is the thought of marrying your child's father truly so abhorrent?"

A tiny vee appeared between her brows. She wasn't as certain in her refusal as she wanted to appear.

"It's not abhorrent. It's… I never really thought about getting married again."

"Why?"

Her nose wrinkled a fraction, enough to let him know that her reasons weren't rooted in memories of marital bliss. He made a mental note to call the private security firm that conducted the checks for all of his employees, ignoring the prick to his conscience. He trusted Clara. He did. But after what he had been through as a child with his father, after years of dealing with Celestine's outrageous behavior, he would not go back through the hell of having another scandal touch his country.

Whether or not he liked it, his future wife's background needed a second look.

"I used to want a family, but then Miles died, I came to work here, and dating has never been a big priority. I guess I assumed my time had passed." She seemed to be choosing her words carefully. "Miles and I were very young when we got married. Too young. We could have made better decisions." Her gaze shifted to him, and steel flashed in her blue gaze. The show of strength sparked the sensual awareness that had never been far out of reach since that night in the gym.

"Many married couples don't enjoy matrimony."

The steel melted into something soft and sad. "Some do." She shook her head. "But you're right. Many couples don't."

"However," Alaric cut in, "I'm not suggesting a marriage based on the lies so many put forth in their over-the-top proposals. It's based on practicality."

"Practicality?"

"Yes. Facts. Marriage would provide our child with a legitimate claim to the throne. It would also extend the protection of this office to both you and our son or daughter."

She frowned. "Protection?"

"I am not without enemies. Marrying me would ensure you and our child are safe."

He stood and circled around his desk. His respect for Clara increased as she stayed where she was, not budging as he sat on the edge of the desk and left just a few inches between himself and her chair.

"What's your plan?"

"I just found out yesterday. I haven't really had time to make a plan."

He pounced. "So you were planning on remaining in the employ of the country of Linnaea? Or staying here and finding a new job?"

Her eyes widened slightly. "I…"

"And am I not to be allowed access to my own child?"

"No, that's not…" She shook her head. "I would never deny you, or my child, their father. I loved my father. I can't imagine not having had him in my life."

The crack widened.

"What about putting our son or daughter to bed? Being there when they skin their knee? Or bring home their first drawing from school?"

Her lips parted. "You… I never pictured you as…"

"A father?" His mouth curved up. "Until yesterday, you never had a reason to."

Pink tinged her cheeks. "True. You're just normally reserved. It's hard to imagine you kissing a child's knee to make it feel better."

"I accepted long ago that any marriage I entered into would be for political reasons." His mother's tear-streaked face gazing out the window flashed in his mind. "Given what I've seen of love and passion, I had no interest in pursuing an alliance with so-called romantic roots. But I knew I would always be the kind of father mine wasn't."

Present, for one, he thought as he stood and walked to the window. How many times had he looked out a window waiting for his father to arrive, for dinner or a trip, only to be left watching as the sky turned from sunset gold to starry darkness? How often had his father chosen the company of a woman he'd just met over that of his own wife and, once she was gone, his own son?

It had been nearly twenty years since the last time he'd allowed himself to be disappointed. Twenty years and he still carried the token with him, wrapped in a red cloth in his billfold.

He'd been a child on the cusp of becoming a man, the ache of his mother's death still fresh. All he'd wanted was one ride on a Ferris wheel with his father. He'd watched the red cars of the Riesenrad from his hotel window, eyes fixed on the lights, ears ringing with the imagined music and laughter of families as they enjoyed the historic ride instead of the ticking of the clock as the minutes turned to hours.

He'd woken up to the sound of Daxon stumbling into the hotel room, a half-murmured apology making it out of his crusty lips before he'd dashed into the bathroom and slammed the door.

Few people could identify the day they had gone from child to adult. His would forever be burned into his memory.

Anger surged through him. Not being married to Clara, not being there for his child, would be walking in his father's footsteps.

"I will be a part of my child's life. That is nonnegotiable."

The words came out much harsher than he'd intended, but he didn't apologize. Clara was not a foolish woman. Even if she didn't know the full story of his painful childhood, she had to comprehend what kind of life could be waiting for a royal child born out of wedlock.

Silence reigned behind him. He waited. He excelled at waiting. He didn't want to hurt Clara, to force her. He wanted her to reach the same conclusion on her own.

But if push came to shove, he would fight.

The soft sigh behind him signaled victory. He stayed at the window.

Wait. Let her come to you.

"What if I agreed to stay in Linnaea? Signed some sort of custody agreement?"

"That does not resolve the issue of legitimacy as it pertains to our child's claim to the throne. Nor," he added as he turned back to face her, "does it solve the problem of the scandal that will rock this country, not to mention Europe, at the news that the future king's illicit liaison with his secretary produced an illegitimate child."

Sparks practically crackled in the air around her as she stood, her hands balled into fists.

"Executive assistant."

"What?"

"I'm *not* a secretary," she ground out. "I'm an executive assistant."

He stalked toward her, savoring the infusion of color in her cheeks, the crackling blue flames in her eyes as she held her ground.

"You type up documents. You answer calls. You manage my schedule." A slow, cocky smile spread across his face. "Sounds like a secretary to me."

She gave him an answering smile, sharp and full of fight. "Is it common practice for you to make love to your *secretaries* on top of your desk?"

The barb found its mark as his anger swelled. He'd been so damned foolish. But, he resolved as he took another step that brought him within inches of her, he would make it right.

"You're the first. Although I wouldn't call that love-making."

One brow shot up. "Oh?"

He leaned in, inhaling the rosy, orange scent tinged with a hint of something woodsy that had become imprinted on his skin that fateful night. The smell of the fresh rose arrangement in the formal dining room had sparked memories of how smooth the skin of her thighs had felt as he'd lifted her onto the desk. A bite of an orange had him reliving the sensation of her lips parting for him, welcoming him into the sweet, hot heat of her mouth as she'd moaned every time he'd thrust into her body.

Their night together may have been impulsive and reckless. But as much as he should regret it, he couldn't. Not when it had felt so damn good.

"That was wild sex. Next time will be different."

She swallowed hard. Her tongue darted out, touching her lower lip in an unconscious gesture as her eyes locked on his.

"You can't seduce me into marrying you, Alaric."

"I'm not. But good sex would be a bonus to our arrangement."

A small laugh escaped as she looked down. He put one finger under her chin and gently but firmly tilted her face back up. At first, he'd wondered if there was something about him preventing Clara from saying yes. But it seemed like her resistance was rooted in something else, something from her past.

"What did Miles do to cause this aversion to marriage?"

The spell broke. The fire disappeared from Clara's eyes as she stepped back, replaced by the flinty hardness she usually exhibited when dealing with everything from an angry ambassador to a reporter caught infiltrating the palace.

"This has nothing to do with Miles, or my former marriage."

"Then what?"

No answer. She just stared at him with that unyielding gaze. It was ridiculous to feel hurt that she wouldn't confide in him, not when he himself loathed sharing any piece of himself beyond what the public saw.

But it did hurt. He had shared a part of himself that night in the gym, when he'd continued to batter the bag and let Clara see him without a shred of dignity as he'd let his emotions show in every punch, every blow.

Now, when the stakes were much higher than a simple holiday dinner gone wrong, when she was pregnant with *his* child, she was holding back from him and making what should have been a cut-and-dried situation tangled and messy.

"Keep your secrets, then, Clara. But if you truly think that you'll be raising our child on your own without my involvement, depriving him or her of his rightful inheritance, then you're not the woman I thought you were."

She flinched. A low blow, he knew, but an accurate one. How could she not see that her plan to be a single mother was a foolish one? Even dangerous when one factored in the threats that royals and dignitaries faced in the world today? She was not a stupid woman. What on earth was possessing her to reject his offer?

"You only want to marry me because you don't want people thinking you're like your father."

His body went cold. Judging by the draining of the color from her face, she knew she'd hit her mark with stinging accuracy.

"Alaric, I'm… I'm sorry…"

Her voice trailed off as he held up a hand.

"Don't apologize. You're right." He crossed to his desk, focusing on the neat stack of papers that required his attention before the end of the day. "Believe it or not, Clara, I truly want to be a part of our child's life. I want it to grow up without the daily pain I lived through. I want it to be safe and know that it's loved."

"And you need an heir," Clara added, a touch of bitterness in her tone. "It makes me feel like a broodmare."

"I do need an heir. But if we don't marry, I will marry someone else. The children I bear with whomever I marry will inherit the throne. Perhaps that won't matter to the child you carry. Or perhaps it will mean everything." He took the top packet of papers and pushed it across the desk. "I will do anything I can to make this arrangement acceptable for you. I've typed up a preliminary marriage contract. My lawyers made every clause in your favor to the best of their ability."

She stared at the contract as if it was a poisonous snake about to bite.

"A contract?"

"Prenuptial agreement. A common practice."

Slowly, she reached out and picked it up. Her eyes darted over the first page, widening with every sentence she read.

"You want us to get married within a week?"

"We're risking exposure of our tryst already with you being a month along. The sooner we get married, the better."

She flipped the page. "A fidelity clause?"

"One thing I have never tolerated is betrayal." Not after what he'd seen his mother go through. Marianne had been faithful to Daxon until her dying day, regardless of the numerous photos and tabloid articles. Each affair had chipped away at her already-fragile heart. She'd seen her commitment as a badge of pride, that she was doing the right thing by the man she'd married. Alaric had been torn between wanting to rage at her for letting Daxon get away with his perfidies and admiration for her grace and class, traits he had tried to emulate over the years.

Until he'd lifted his secretary onto his desk and ravished her like a wild animal.

"That clause goes both ways. You'll never have to be concerned about me straying. There's also a handsome allowance, the freedom to come and go from Linnaea as you wish."

One hand slowly went up to her forehead, the tiniest tremor visible in her fingers.

"I… I need time to think."

He looked down so she couldn't see the triumph in his eyes. They had gone from her stalwart refusal to considering his offer. He'd conducted enough business to know that if she had already started to reevaluate, it was only a matter of time before she gave in completely.

"I'll see you tomorrow morning, then. Ten a.m. again?"

He expected her to argue, to dig her heels in and ask for more time. But when he looked up, she merely nodded.

"Ten a.m."

And then she was gone, the door closing softly behind her. Instead of feeling exhilarated, he felt surprisingly bereft. Yes, he wanted to achieve his goals. But, he realized with a small amount of surprise, he wanted Clara to be happy, too.

He gave himself a mental shake. Given the past seven years and all he'd come to learn about Clara, from her spine of steel when dealing with feuding politicians to her deft handling of his father's antics, if she truly didn't want to get married to him she wouldn't have started to consider his proposal.

Better, he decided, not to look a gift horse in the mouth. By the end of the week, Clara Stephenson would be his wife, and another crisis would be averted.

CHAPTER SIX

CLARA GLANCED AT her wristwatch. Nine fifty-two. Twenty-four hours had passed far too quickly. Focusing on work for most of the day had kept the swirling mess of her personal life at bay. It had been a blessing until exhaustion hit her like a truck. She'd barely staggered up to her room, where she'd collapsed onto the couch and slept until a quarter past six in the morning.

Which had left her with less than four hours to make the biggest decision of her life.

Yesterday had thrown her for a loop. She had assumed Alaric's interest in marriage had been solely motivated by securing an heir to the throne. But he'd surprised her. Again. Alaric wanted to be a father. With that sentiment, he'd started a crack in the wall she'd built, a crack that had only widened over the course of their conversation.

She'd grown up wanting a family of her own. The more time she'd spent with Miles and his family, however, the more that desire had mutated into a commitment to not bring a child into the frigid atmosphere of the Clemont family. Temperance and Stanley would have inserted themselves into her child's life, ensuring he or she was raised as they saw fit. Miles had said he wanted children when they dated. But how could he possibly have had a child when he still acted like one himself?

The face he'd made when she'd try to take the keys from him that night, when she'd begged him to let her drive, had reminded her of a toddler not getting his way.

"Don't tell me what to do!" he'd shouted before he'd backhanded her across the face.

Her hand drifted up to her cheek. Miles hadn't left a permanent mark, but his tantrums and self-indulgences had left plenty of wounds invisible to the naked eye.

In the years since Miles's death, she had kept people at arm's length, including potential friends and prospective romances. Marriage and children had been even further down the list of things she saw in her future. She wasn't a fool to believe that all men were so horrible. But she was a fool when it came to her own judgment. She'd made such a colossal error with Miles. What if she made another one with Alaric?

Another glance at her watch. Nine fifty-six.

Alaric was a good man in many ways. She knew that he was right, that marrying him would ensure the best possible future for their child.

But what about them? Could she really commit herself to another loveless marriage? He'd made it perfectly clear yesterday that it would be a business arrangement, another point in favor of the argument that she had read far more into their relationship of the past year. Yet the way he'd spoken about being a father...she wanted that for her child. She'd been so blessed to grow up with a father who had adored her. She'd lost a piece of herself when he'd died. Could she truly deny her son or daughter the chance to have a father like Alaric, one she sensed would fight for and love and care for them just as much as her own father had? All because she'd made mistakes in the past and was now letting her own fears and insecurities influence her decision?

And then there was the glaring fact that, if it did come out that Alaric had gotten his executive assistant pregnant, it could undo some of the considerable progress he'd achieved over the last few weeks. From stripping Daxon of his power to distancing himself from Celestine's antics just as Switzerland had agreed to throw both its support and its treasury behind the palace, Linnaea had made more advancements in just over a month than it had in the years she'd been working here.

Alaric always placed the country first. It was a role he'd been born to, and one he'd accepted long ago. She'd always worked with Linnaea's best interests at heart. She loved the country, the people.

But could she do the same as Alaric? Commit her entire life to the throne?

Her head dropped back against the wall with a dull thud. Instead of walking into this meeting with answers, all she had was more questions.

The numbers changed to ten o'clock. She stood, crossed the hall and knocked. Movements she did every day. But right now, she felt like she was moving through a dream, each gesture sluggish.

It didn't help that Alaric had changed the location of their meeting from his office to his private apartment.

If he'd been trying to throw her off, he'd succeeded far too easily.

The door opened. Alaric towered over her, his face the same inscrutable mask he always wore, his emerald eyes dark and flinty.

Her heart thudded in her chest. Before that night in the gym, she'd acknowledged Alaric's handsomeness. He was, and always had been, devastatingly attractive. So were the abs on Michelangelo's statue of David. That didn't mean she was going to fall head over heels for a hunk of marble, living or not. Alaric had been handsome but cold, a leader who placed his people first but also ruthless when it came to decision-making. She had carried out his orders on more than one occasion while privately disagreeing with how he'd gone about it. He eschewed any type of emotion over logic, facts and data.

Seeing him as she'd seen him the night of the failed Christmas dinner—raw, rough, wild—had turned her appreciation into red-hot longing.

It hadn't just changed her physical attraction to him. He'd started to ask for her opinion more, confide to her the reasons behind his decisions. She'd glimpsed so much more of the man behind the prince. Here was a man who truly wanted the best for his people, who didn't want to make the mistakes of his predecessor who had made his decisions purely on emotion. She still didn't agree with his borderline obsession with keeping all feelings out of his choices. But she'd understood him better, respected his reasons and silently thanked the powers that be that her silly infatuation would never go beyond her own fantasies where she could risk getting her heart broken.

Then he'd looked at her, eyes alight with molten emerald fire, and she'd burned for him.

And now she was carrying his child. She was carrying his child and, she acknowledged as she walked into his apartment, she owed it to her child to give it everything she could. Including a father.

Her eyes wandered before she could stop herself. His suite was triple the size of hers, with floor-to-ceiling windows overlooking the mountains and a balcony facing the lake. Brown leather furniture trimmed in brass, thick burgundy carpets and drapes that made the room feel surprisingly cozy and a couple of carefully selected paintings of Linnaean landscapes.

She turned to find him watching her. She returned his frank gaze, concealing her surprise at the comfortable home he'd created for himself.

"Did you sleep well?" he asked as he gestured to a chair in front of the fireplace, a thick blanket draped over one arm. She sat, resisting the beckoning warmth of the crackling flames and the buttery soft leather as she watched him sit across from her.

"As well as I could."

The tiniest quirk of his lips made something twist in her chest. Alaric's equivalent of throwing his head back and laughing. When she'd seen its appearance in various meetings over the years, it had always made her inwardly chuckle. Over the last year, she'd seen it more, chalked it up as a sign of their growing camaraderie that he was sharing something so simple and yet so important with her, a piece of himself no one else got to see.

"Before you tell me what decision stole your sleep, I'd like to share something with you." He reached out and grabbed something red off the end table next to his chair. He unwrapped the brightly colored fabric to reveal a small coin.

"Are you offering to buy my hand in marriage?"

"If I was into such outdated methods of persuading a woman to marry me, I would be offering far more than this." He stood, crossed the room and placed the coin in her hand. She peered closer. It was gold, the edges slightly worn, the image smoothed out by time and wear, as if the owner had taken it out of their pocket and touched it, tracing the delicate features of the Ferris wheel emblazoned on one side. On the other, elegant script read Riesenrad.

"The Ferris wheel in Vienna?"

She looked up to see Alaric's gaze fixated not on her but the coin, a naked pain in his eyes that shocked her.

"My father took me with him to Vienna after my mother died. I was fourteen." He turned away, shoving his hands into his pockets as he walked over to the windows and looked out over his domain. With his shoulders thrown back and his suit tailored to follow every hard line of his muscular body, he looked every inch the future king.

"It was the one time I remember him trying to be a father. He was in town for a conference and took me out to lunch, walks around Vienna between meetings. It was the most time we'd spent together. It made me think that perhaps my mother's death had changed things. On our last night, we were supposed to ride the Riesenrad."

A weight settled on Clara's shoulders, Alaric's pain seeping into her own body.

"I had a view of it from our hotel. I sat by the window

for five hours, sure that he would walk in any moment and we would go." She sensed rather than saw the hurt pulsing through his body, tightening his muscles further as he tried to keep his emotions under control. "It was after midnight when he stumbled in drunk. He'd had a glass of wine at a reception, then another at dinner, and then he just didn't stop. He spent the evening with the wife of a dignitary."

What was there to say? Everything that came to mind seemed trite, meant to fill the silence versus offer genuine comfort. She had never experienced anything so horrific from her parents. Her marriage may have been a disaster, but her parents' union had been one for the storybooks, a relationship built on mutual respect and a deep-seated love.

And her father…her eyes grew hot. He'd been wonderful. Not perfect, but she had never doubted he'd loved her. He'd taken her to carnivals, on nature walks, had read to her at night and rocked her back to sleep when thunderstorms had spooked her.

What would it be like to have a father who not only didn't show any love or affection, but literally abandoned their grieving child in their hour of need?

The ache that had started yesterday when Alaric pointed out that not marrying meant her child would grow up without a regular presence from a father figure burst and filled her chest. She knew she would be a great mother. But if she had the chance to offer her child the kind of life she had had, one with a father who cared for them, would it be selfish to deny them that?

She rose and walked across the room. Alaric didn't move, didn't even show that he registered her approach, until she tentatively moved her hand from her stomach to his shoulder. His body flinched but he didn't move, didn't look at her. Slowly her hand relaxed, her fingers splaying across the soft material of his jacket.

How long they stayed like that, she couldn't say. Each moment stretched into the next, awkwardness gradually easing into a familiarity, a comforting space where they could both exist in their pain and confusion without having to fill the silence.

Her heart thudded. Alaric didn't want love. She wasn't sure she did, either. Her one attempt at love had meant relinquishing so much of herself. But this…perhaps this type of understanding would be enough.

Words rose to her lips. Alaric had confided so much in her. If she was truly contemplating saying yes, he deserved to know the truth of what had happened that night: the role she'd played in her husband's death. The threats Temperance Clemont had leveled at her before she'd left for the final time, to ensure Clara never found happiness with anyone again.

The words died on her tongue. The Clemonts hadn't been a part of her life for eight years. If they had truly wanted to sabotage her, they would have made a move before now. What was the point in bringing it up? Besides, she was already pregnant with the heir to Linnaea's throne. If she brought up the past now, it would introduce the possibility of scandal just as Alaric was finally distancing himself from his father's and fiancée's tumultuous pasts.

That's just an excuse, a nasty little voice whispered in her ear. *You're afraid.*

Her fingers tensed, pressed harder on his shoulder.

Alaric was too lost in his own past to notice. Slowly, she eased her touch, relaxing her hand and breathing in deeply.

Yes, she was afraid. Afraid that if she told Alaric what had truly happened that night, he would look at her in disgust, the way he'd looked every time he'd seen a picture of his fiancée or had a confrontation with Daxon.

Every time he had to confront a *scandal*.

Finally, he turned. Her hand dropped and she stepped back, giving them both some much-needed distance.

"Do you keep the coin to remind yourself of his true character?"

Alaric's dark chuckle made coldness slither down her spine. She would never want to be on the receiving end of Prince Alaric Van Ambrose's wrath. The world was fortunate that he had chosen to use his razor-sharp intelligence and formidable will for good.

"I have plenty of reminders as to his nature. No, I kept it for my child." He plucked the coin from her hand and held it in his own, gazing at it for a long moment before he brought his arresting green gaze up and met her eyes. "As a reminder to myself to be a better father than mine ever was. As a reminder that something as simple as a ride on the Ferris wheel can mean more than all the sports cars and fancy suits and money in the world to a child."

His words ripped away the last vestiges of her initial refusal. She swallowed hard, turned away from him and walked back over to her chair. She didn't sit, ran her fingers over the soft leather. The touch grounded her, gave her something visual to focus on other than him.

"Then our child should count themself lucky to have you as a father."

Silence descended on the room. Her fingers drifted down to the arm of the chair, tapped the brass buttons embedded in the material as she waited for him to reply.

Then, at last: "Is that an answer?"

She nodded, unable to speak past the lump in her throat. She had no idea if she was doing the right thing. So many questions and worries swirled in her mind. Would she and Alaric be able to make a marriage work? What if she wasn't a good queen? Even though she was not a Linnaean national, the country and its people had become very dear to her in the time she'd spent in the palace. The possibility that she would let them down just as they were finally clawing their way out of the darkness made her sick to her stomach.

And the baby…the most important aspect of this whole arrangement. Was this the right thing for her baby?

The man didn't even blink, just returned her nod with one of his own as if he had expected nothing less.

"Review this and sign it by this evening."

Her first proposal had gone very differently. Miles had proposed on bended knee at one of his parents' grand parties in front of several hundred guests, sliding the three-carat diamond ring on her finger as if it was the Hope Diamond and basking in the congratulations the guests bestowed on them throughout the evening. It hadn't felt like a proposal rooted in love. No, it had all been for show. Just like Miles, as she'd come to learn the hard way.

She'd always sworn that if she ever got married again,

it would be very different. Who knew that it would be transactional, a signing of papers and a few exchanged words for the sake of legality and legacy instead of any romantic notions?

Perhaps this is better, her rational side consoled her. *There's no false hope. No ideas of love to let you down. You know exactly what you're getting.*

"You said yesterday you wanted to get married by the end of the week."

"Yes. I'll arrange for the ceremony to take place on Saturday." He pulled his phone out of his pocket and began to type something. "We'll prepare a small statement to be released after we've departed for a month-long honeymoon. I don't want to detract from my sister's wedding."

A small smile tugged at her lips. It had been nice to see Alaric finally grow close to someone, especially someone like Briony, who had taken on her duties as princess with incredible aplomb despite having grown up across the ocean in a small town in Kansas.

"She'll appreciate the thought."

"It will also keep the spotlight on her and off the timeline of recent events."

Her smile disappeared. She should have thought of that, would have thought of it if her mind had been in the right place.

"A wise approach."

"The new public relations officer will handle the details of the press release."

"New officer?"

"I promoted your assistant, Meira, this morning."

The walls of her invisible prison shuddered, pressed in on her as her mouth dropped open.

"Meira?"

"Yes."

"But… I don't understand."

Alaric looked up from his phone and frowned. "What is there to understand? I will need to hire a new executive assistant. I offered Meira both your role and that of public relations officer. She chose the latter."

"Without talking to me first?"

The frown deepened. "I make decisions about palace staffing, Clara. I have for years."

The reprimand brought back the sharp sting in her cheeks from Miles's slap all those years ago.

"I should have been consulted."

"A minor change in staffing hardly seemed worth bothering you over."

Her mouth opened, closed, opened again.

"What if I had said no?"

He glanced up at her again with his eyes narrowed. "I told you yesterday, no wasn't an option. I made my decisions based on what the best choice was for everyone. Given your history, I knew you'd come to the same conclusion."

She pressed her lips together so he couldn't see her gnashing her teeth. She didn't know what ticked her off more, that he knew what decision she would make before she had or that he'd started making plans before she'd told him yes.

He must have sensed her consternation because he folded his arms across his chest.

"You told me yourself Meira wanted to eventually

move into a public relations role. I listened and I offered her that opportunity." His phone pinged, drawing his attention off her. "Meira is working on the press release now. I'll send the details regarding the actual ceremony to you this evening along with the paperwork."

She tried to keep her tone calm as she voiced the fear slowly unfurling in her belly. "Am I to have all my responsibilities stripped from me then?"

Alaric blinked in surprise before a frown crinkled his brow. "No. I would hope you'd think better of me than that, Clara, after all our years together. You've seen how much of a role Briony has taken on as princess. Once we've navigated these first few weeks, we'll sit down to discuss what duties you'll have as queen." The frown deepened. "I have no interest in having a queen who is nothing more than an ornament. But we're to be married. You can't continue as my assistant."

She wanted to stay and argue. But what was the point? Meira had told her multiple times how much she wanted to work in the public relations office. She had become a dear friend, the first true friend Clara had had in years. She couldn't torpedo something Meira had been working toward just because she didn't like how it had come about. And Alaric's explanation for reassigning her duties made sense. She hadn't really thought about how her role in the palace would change, but it would need to change. She'd seen all the things Briony had taken on since she'd come to Linnaea. The to-do list for the future queen of the country would most likely be even longer and more intense.

Rational reasons for why he'd done what he'd done. None of it assuaged her growing annoyance with Alaric's princely manner. Had she thought his firm decision-making attractive before?

Because right now, it was just irritating.

She moved toward the door. She'd barely taken five steps before Alaric stepped in front of her.

"Clara."

Slowly, she looked up. Her gaze landed on his lips as her irritation melted away. Did he want to kiss her again? The thought left butterflies dancing in her stomach despite her frustration, anticipatory flutters mixed with a nervous quivering of what a kiss would mean. A gesture to seal the deal? A premonition of the intimacy to come? He'd certainly made his preferences for both fidelity and physical affection clear yesterday. But she thought she'd have time, time to get used to the idea of being married again, of being married to her *boss*, before they would touch again.

Because deep down, if she was being honest with herself, it hadn't just been her failed marriage to Miles or the circumstances around their child being conceived that had held her back from saying yes. No, it was how Alaric had made her feel when they'd made love, how sexy and beautiful and alive he'd made her feel as she'd come apart in his arms. The sensations had been so intense, so raw, had made her feel like her heart had been laid bare for him to see every bit of herself. Something she'd never experienced before, and certainly not one she had ever expected to experience with Alaric.

But to let someone who held so much power gain access to her body, let alone her heart, was terrifying. What if she couldn't keep him at arm's length? What if she made the same mistakes she had with Miles?

What if, what if, what if...?

"I'm very tired, Your Highness. Could we continue this discussion later?"

He knew she was lying. The man had a built-in lie detector, had used it to eject plenty of unscrupulous and deceitful business professionals, politicians and royals from various meetings over the years she'd worked for him. But right now, she didn't care. She just wanted to get away, to be alone with her tumultuous thoughts.

His hand came up, his fingers settling lightly on her jaw. She inhaled sharply.

"If you call me Alaric."

The smugness in his tone told her he knew exactly the kind of effect he was having on her, the heat that bloomed on her skin where his fingertips rested.

She narrowed her eyes. "Why?"

"I'm to be your husband. When we're in private, using my given name is appropriate."

"You're not my husband yet."

Something flashed in his eyes but disappeared before she could discern what it was.

"You said it once before."

Her entire body flushed. She had said it more than once. Moaned it, borderline screamed it into his mouth as he'd sealed his lips over hers to smother her cry of ecstasy as he'd brought her to a level of exquisite pleasure she'd never experienced.

"I'd like to leave now, Alaric."

No sooner had his name left her lips then he stepped back. Cool air brushed her skin before embarrassed heat replaced the warmth from his touch. He was much more in command of himself than she was.

The what-ifs grew stronger as she brushed past him. She had made it to the door, her hand reaching for the knob, when his voice rang out once more.

"Is there anything else you want to share with me before we make this official?"

Don't panic. He can't possibly know you were there that night. That Miles is dead because of you.

She looked over her shoulder at him as casually as she could manage, striving to keep her panic buried. Part of her wanted nothing more than to confide in him, to finally unburden herself. Logically, she knew she hadn't intended for Miles to get hurt, let alone die.

But logic didn't banish her guilt. She had been the one to let him drive, who had let her embarrassment when he'd slapped her overcome common sense as he'd gotten behind the wheel and she'd climbed in the car with him. And ultimately it had been her actions that had led to the car accident that had claimed his life. She'd been weak when she needed to be strong. Because of that moment of weakness, a man was dead, a son buried in the ground. No matter how much she loathed Temperance and Stanley Clemont, their grief had been real.

The truth had stayed buried this long, survived Alaric's notoriously in-depth background checks and the lens of the paparazzi so frequently fixed on Linnaea's royal family. There was nothing to gain by sharing it now.

Nothing to gain and everything to lose.

"No." She forced a smile to her face. "Nothing."

CHAPTER SEVEN

THE DAY OF her wedding dawned bright and beautiful. Sapphire-blue sky, glittering white snow, and a lull in the brisk winter wind that had whipped down from the mountains and shrieked its way through the castle gardens the past few days.

Any other bride would have been ecstatic. Clara, however, could barely stand to look at her own reflection in the mirror. She stood at the window of her suite, her last night in the apartment she'd called home for the past seven years, her fingers resting on the cold glass of the window.

She'd tossed and turned all night. Was she doing the right thing? Should she tell Alaric about Miles? The accident? Could she make a loveless marriage work?

Yet if she did change her mind, told Alaric she couldn't go through with the wedding...where would that leave her? Her child? She'd be trading one set of problems for another.

"You look beautiful, Your Highness."

Clara forced a smile onto her face as she turned to Meira Laird, her former assistant and now officially the new public relations officer. The petite raven-haired young woman had come across as timid and shy when Clara had first met her a year ago when she interviewed her for the position of executive assistant to the executive assistant of the prince. Her quiet, compassionate nature concealed a talent for communication. It was why Clara had mentioned Meira's interest in public relations to Alaric.

She just hadn't anticipated Alaric moving forward without talking to her first.

In a matter of days, their relationship had drastically changed. As his executive assistant, she had felt respected. Alaric consulted her, asked for her opinions and, most importantly, listened to her.

Yet between his push to get married so quickly and now making changes in her staffing without talking to her, was the camaraderie and rapport they'd developed over the years going to be replaced by a dictator who made decisions for her? Her career had given her purpose after her unwanted time as a trophy wife. Who would she be without it?

An image of Miles's face appeared in her mind. Handsome, yes, made even more attractive by tucks and nips since he'd been in college. She'd been so lost after her mother's death, being truly alone in the world for the first time, that she hadn't noticed the signs until his ring was on her finger.

Not true. No, she had noticed in the months leading up to the wedding. Had felt uncomfortable with how he discouraged her from befriending anyone he didn't introduce her to. But she had wanted so desperately to be happy, to have the kind of marriage her parents had

had, to not be alone, that she had looked the other way, gone along with his suggestions to avoid conflict.

Panic fluttered low in her belly. Was she doing the same thing now?

"You look a thousand miles away."

Clara shook her head and focused on Meira.

"I am," she confessed with a smile. "Sorry."

The few people Miles had allowed her to be friends with had snubbed their noses at her once she'd gotten rid of the Clemont name. Trusting others, let alone herself, had been a challenge. Becoming close with Meira had been a saving grace she didn't even know she needed. She'd finally started to relax and enjoy life outside of work again. How quickly she'd come to trust and feel comfortable around Briony had been a result of her friendship with Meira, too.

What if her marriage to Alaric altered her relationship with Meira, too? What if she withdrew into herself and lost so much of the progress she'd made?

Meira approached her and slid an arm around her shoulders, giving her a comforting squeeze.

"This is different. He's different."

She'd confessed some of the details of her first marriage to Meira over the summer after one too many glasses of wine. Meira had returned the favor by sharing her own story of heartbreak, a young man she'd fallen in love with who had deserted her when her family had lost their fortune. The summer night revelations had bonded the two women.

"He's different in some ways," Clara agreed. "But if I wasn't carrying his child, we wouldn't be getting married."

Meira's eyes narrowed thoughtfully as she stepped back and smoothed the skirt of Clara's dress.

"I'm not so sure about that."

Clara turned away so Meira wouldn't see her rolling her eyes. Meira had been just as trepidatious as Clara about relationships until Briony and Cass had descended on the palace and surprised everyone by falling in love. Planning the royal wedding had brought on a severe case of romanticism.

"I am."

In the mirror she caught Meira's head shaking.

"I think you two have been mistaking respect and admiration for something more."

Clara laughed.

"What on earth are you talking about?"

"The way you two look at each other. How His Highness..." Meira's hands fluttered in the air for a moment as she tried to find the right words. "Softens around you. It's subtle, but it's there. He's more relaxed around you, and I don't think it's just because he respects your work."

She'd thought so, too. But based on how quickly he'd shifted back into being prince, how rapidly he'd decided her opinion didn't matter now that they were engaged, Alaric reserved his more personal interactions for friends or close acquaintances, not lovers or fiancées. It had been eight years since she'd been touched so intimately, and the only time in her life she'd enjoyed physical pleasure. Of course she would have a physical reaction to a man who could make her feel like that.

But romance? Emotional intimacy? No. Even she couldn't be so stupid as to make the same mistake twice and fall for a man who would never be capable of loving her. It was absurd to even contemplate the power-wielding, strict prince as having anything approaching romantic feelings for anyone. The few affairs he'd conducted when she'd first worked for him had seemed transactional, cold, businesslike. She'd booked enough dinner reservations and sent calendar invites to his paramours via email to know the man didn't approach relationships with romantic intent.

He may have been the best lover she'd ever been with—although she only had the one to compare with, and that wasn't saying much—but sex and love were two very different things.

She glanced at her reflection in the mirror and bit back a sigh. Not exactly the dress she'd envisioned a member of royalty wearing. She'd picked a cream-colored sheath dress with long sleeves. Simple, elegant, a far cry from the full-skirted gown Temperance Clemont had insisted she wear. Clara had wanted so badly to have a relationship with Miles's mother that she'd gone along with her future mother-in-law. The tulle of the underskirt had made her itch, and she hadn't been able to eat a bite of the lemon lobster fettucine because she'd been terrified of dropping food on the five-figure dress.

Still…she'd always thought that if she got married again, she would make sure it was in a dress she wanted.

Her eyes drifted to her window and the rooftops of the buildings of Eira, the city she'd come to call home. When she'd first started, Daxon's frequent appearances in the international tabloids had struck her as unprofessional and annoying. But as she'd dug deeper into her new career and been confronted with the full scope of the damage he'd caused, from the lack of affordable housing and quality jobs to damaged relationships with countries across the world that wanted nothing to do with a king who preferred to spend money versus rule, her work had become very personal to her. It had physically hurt to see deals fall through after one of Daxon's affairs was splashed across Instagram or to hear conversation about Celestine's latest tabloid feature dominate a conference instead of one of Alaric's carefully crafted economic proposals.

Shame crept up her neck and turned her cheeks red. She turned away from the mirror. What kind of queen was she going to be if she was feeling sorry for herself over a damned dress? Yes, things were looking up for Linnaea. A wedding dress for a future queen who never should have been queen in the first place was definitely not a priority.

With her focus back where it needed to be, Clara moved toward her bed to grab her coat.

"It's nearly time. We should head down."

Meira sighed. "I know he wants to keep this a secret and give Briony a little more time in the spotlight, but couldn't he have at least picked somewhere a tiny bit more romantic than his office?"

"It's not in his office anymore."

Meira's head whipped around as she narrowed her eyes.

"Oh?"

"It's in the rose garden."

She tried, and failed, to keep her voice neutral. Alaric's text that morning sharing the new location had surprised her, too. She hadn't been able to deny the slight thrill that had pulsed through her at the thoughtful gesture, even if it had also confused her to no end. Was there a reason behind his sudden change of heart? Or was he simply trying to do something nice for his future wife?

A knock sounded on the door. Meira answered, murmured something to the person on the other side and turned back with a pale blue box in her hands, the lid topped off with a white bow.

"A footman just delivered this." Her voice held a touch of smugness as she gestured to the small white card on top. "Guess who it's from?"

"I can guess," Clara replied drily even as her heartbeat kicked up a notch. What could Alaric have sent her?

Meira set the box on a table. Clara lifted the lid and peeled back the tissue paper. Even she was unable to contain her gasp of surprise.

"Are those…"

Meira's voice trailed off as Clara let her fingers glide over the different materials inside. Her earlier excitement returned as a smile broke across her face.

"Wedding dresses."

Alaric glanced down at his watch. Two minutes to noon and no sign of his bride-to-be. Did the dress not fit? Had she misunderstood which garden? Or, worse, had she changed her mind and fled the palace?

Stop. He never questioned himself like this. He had not pulled the country back from the brink of financial disaster by engaging in self-doubt. There was a solution for every problem. No matter what happened today, he would fix it.

He focused on the looming escallonia hedges that surrounded the palace rose garden. In the dead of winter, the glossy leaves still held on to their green, a welcome splash of color beneath the snow. Come springtime, white and pale pink flowers would blossom, followed a couple months later by an explosion of color as the roses bloomed.

A more appropriate setting for a wedding, he grudgingly acknowledged. Briony had poked her head into his office last night. Despite his attempts at keeping his upcoming nuptials under wraps, his sister had found out and somehow knew about the baby, too. How, she'd refused to say, but his concern that she might be upset over her spotlight being stolen so quickly after her own wedding was invalid. Briony had been thrilled, pattering on about gaining a brother, a husband, a sister-in-law, and now a niece or nephew in such a short time.

Well, thrilled to a point. Once she'd learned of his plans for the ceremony to take place in his office, she'd nearly leaped across hid desk and strangled him.

"Seriously?" she'd cried. "Clara is carrying your child and you're going to marry her in your *office*?"

It had also been Briony's idea to surprise Clara with three wedding dresses from a designer in downtown Eira.

"She doesn't get to have a real wedding, Alaric. The least you can do is make it memorable for her."

Briony had a point. And it had given him the idea to summon the photographer from the palace's public relations office. Clara could have photos of the ceremony and, when news of their wedding came to light, he could produce the photos to combat negative press. The public loved royal weddings. With the right spin, an elopement in the rose garden would rise above malicious gossip.

He was about to glance down at his watch again when he caught movement out of the corner of his eye. He looked up and froze.

Clara walked down the path toward him. The dress she'd picked, an ivory creation made of lace, clung to her svelte figure before gently flaring out around her knees and cascading into a train that made her seem like she was gliding down the path. A brilliant blue peacoat brought out the color of her eyes and made her pale gold hair glimmer against the backdrop of the snow.

She looked stunning. Like a future queen. When she drew alongside him, he reached out and tucked her gloved hand in the crook of his arm.

She smiled up at him, her eyes soft and glowing.

"Thank you," she whispered. "It's all so lovely."

Satisfaction warmed his chest even as shame threatened to snatch it away. Briony had been right. Two simple gestures had made all the difference in the demeanor of his bride.

As the judge began to speak, Clara's fingers tightened around his arm. He glanced at her. Her eyes were focused on the judge, her face smooth and her lips set in the barest hint of a smile. Despite her gratitude, there was nothing to suggest she thought of this marriage as anything more than what it was: an arrangement to provide protection for her and their child, as well as a secure path to the throne for his heir.

Why did that bother him?

Because, he realized as the judge continued to speak on the sanctity of marriage, that part of him that had been disappointed by Clara's resigned acceptance of her fate was also now longing for something…more. What exactly, he couldn't begin to fathom.

He blinked, realizing the judge was addressing him.

"…take this woman to be your lawfully wedded wife…"

He needed to take a step back from the emotional precipice he'd stumbled onto. Yes, the situation had turned out far better than he had anticipated. But it had still been the result of his loss of control. This was not a fairy-tale royal romance. It was a business arrangement meant to protect an innocent child and the future of the country.

As he slid the wedding band onto Clara's finger, he steeled himself against any further sentimental indulgences. Now was the time to reassume the mantle of leader and focus on what mattered most: guiding his country into a new chapter while preparing to become a father to the next heir to the throne.

He met Clara's gaze and gave her a small, aloof smile.

"I do."

CHAPTER EIGHT

CLARA LOOKED DOWN for the seventh or eighth time since the ceremony at the simple silver band on her left finger. It was official. She was now Clara Van Ambrose, Royal Princess of Linnaea.

Wife.

Not a title she had expected to have anytime in the near future, if ever, and certainly not with Alaric.

Alaric. Her boss. Her *husband.*

After their wedding ceremony, they had posed for a few photos for one of the palace photographers. Another gesture that, despite her best efforts, had further erased some of her concerns and questions and replaced it with hope. Foolish, bright, lovely hope.

She'd barely caught her breath on the elevator ride up to his private quarters.

Their private quarters, she'd amended as she'd walked into them for the second time that week, a nervous fluttering in her chest. Alaric had hinted that their marriage would, in time, include physical intimacy. But surely he hadn't meant now?

No, she'd realized with a mixture of relief and disappointment as he'd given her a slight, distracted smile and then immediately hopped on his phone once the door had closed behind them. It was to prepare for their honeymoon to Lake Geneva. A honeymoon that, judging by his side of the conversation, was all about privacy and giving Alaric the ability to work.

Work that didn't include her anymore.

Less than an hour later, he'd escorted her down to one of the private cars he preferred over the luxurious limousine Daxon liked to ride in. The short ride to the airport had been spent with him switching back and forth between his phone and his laptop as she sat there. The couple of times she'd tried to jump in like she had as his executive assistant, to offer a reminder on upcoming legislation or a detail about a dignitary, he'd told her to stop working and relax.

"You're a princess, not my assistant."

He hadn't said the words cruelly, but they'd still cut deep. Was this what her new life was to be like? Just sitting around like some useless ornament for him to trot out whenever he needed?

Anger simmered below the surface on the one-hour-long private plane ride to Geneva. She never would have guessed by the way he'd welcomed Briony and her activism with Linnaea's education system that he would relegate his wife to the role of fancy bauble.

She couldn't help but wonder if it wasn't how he felt about the role of his wife, but how he felt about *her*. Despite the position she'd served in for the past seven years, she was essentially a commoner, the daughter of a mechanic and a teacher who had only landed in the upper echelons of society because she'd caught Miles's eye. Did Alaric think her capable of organizing his budget and typing his emails, but not of leading the country together?

By the time the plane landed at the airport, she wanted nothing more than to tell him she'd made a mistake, run to the nearest terminal and board the quickest flight home.

Except she had no home. She couldn't just go back to her apartment at the palace. The house she'd lived in with her parents outside of Southampton until her mother's death had been sold long ago to pay for the last of her university tuition. Both her parents had been single children, their parents dead before she'd even been born.

All she had left now was the man descending the stairs onto the tarmac—her husband—and the unplanned child growing inside her. Would it be her only one? Would she continue in her parents' stead?

It was enough, she decided morosely as he turned to hold out his hand to her, to make one thoroughly depressed.

Alaric glanced out the window as the helicopter he'd arranged to take him and his new wife to the lake house slowly descended onto the helipad.

His wife.

No need to get sentimental, he reminded himself. That didn't stop protectiveness from rearing its head as her fingers settled in his and she alighted from the helicopter. Her eyes widened as she took in the sight of the chalet.

"It's beautiful, Alaric."

His hand tightened around hers for a moment before

he forced himself to ease his grip. It was the first time she'd spontaneously used his name. It shouldn't matter.

Didn't matter, he reminded himself as he guided her down the stone path from the helipad toward the house.

"The one purchase my mother oversaw. She spent a lot of time here."

The two-story mansion had been built in a private cove with a private beach on Lake Geneva. His mother had fallen in love with the shingled, pale blue exterior and white shutters adorning each window. The color was too bright for his taste, but he'd never been able to bring himself to change it.

As an added bonus, Daxon despised the place. It didn't matter that the house boasted six bedrooms, an indoor pool and five acres of lakefront real estate. Daxon had berated his wife for choosing a house that looked like it "belonged in a tiny town in Maine" and not in the holdings of a king of Europe. It had been one of the few times his mother had stood up to Daxon. Daxon had retaliated by purchasing a lavish home on Lake Como in Italy and dragging them there for a vacation at least once a year.

However, he reflected as the blades of the helicopter came to a stop and he looked out over the snow-covered grounds leading down to the water's edge, the marble floors and Greek columns of the Lake Como house had always felt more like a museum than a house. Despite his loyalty to Linnaea, even the palace had at times seemed like a prison, his future written before he'd even been born.

Here, in what Daxon had sneeringly referred to as

"the cottage," had been the closest to home he had ever experienced.

It was, he realized with a small degree of surprise, the first time he had ever brought a woman here.

He glanced at Clara out of the corner of his eye. She'd been extremely quiet since they'd flown out of Eira. At first the silence had been welcome. Between delegating how best to use the funds provided by his brother-in-law's deposit into Linnaea's treasury and navigating the upcoming treaty with Switzerland, his list continued to grow.

Somewhere over France the silence had started to creep under his skin. Given Celestine's behavior and frequent portrayals in the media, he'd accepted over the years that when he finally did marry, his queen would do best by staying in the background of official duties. He knew plenty of royals and dignitaries whose significant others excelled at spending money, wearing the latest couture and providing heirs while keeping as far away from their spouses' official duties as possible.

But Clara had never been one to stay in the background. No, she'd surprised him from her first day when she'd flatly told him an email he'd dictated to her was too abrupt. He'd been so surprised by her critique that instead of firing her, he'd asked her what she would change. The resulting second draft had not only been much better, but had led to an improved relationship with the member of Parliament he'd been writing to.

So why, he asked himself, as the pilot circled around the helicopter and opened the door, had he shut her down on the way to the plane? She was a woman who done nothing but work tirelessly for his country, who had agreed to marry him to provide the best possible life for their child even when marriage to him had clearly not been her first choice.

Yet he was treating her exactly like he would have Celestine. The realization left a bitter taste in his mouth. But how could they possibly return to their camaraderie of the previous year? It had been pleasant, yes, but once the constraints keeping them in their proper roles had been removed, they'd lost control so quickly.

He'd lost control.

Just like his father.

His fingers moved across the keyboard, each tap a little more forceful than the last. Clara didn't even glance at him, her eyes trained on the winter landscape outside.

"My mother purchased this when I was ten."

"It's beautiful."

Beneath the monotone he detected a hint of genuine appreciation. A tightness eased inside his chest. He had been concerned about what she would think about the cottage, he realized.

"I didn't ask you about a honeymoon. I just picked the best location for privacy."

Clara shrugged, still not looking at him.

"I understand."

Disappointment unfurled inside him. He didn't like this Clara—agreeable, bland, quiet. Yet he had been the one to shut her down in the car. He had taken her off all of her assignments, initiated the hiring process for a new executive assistant and planned their honeymoon without asking for her opinion.

An apology rose to his lips. The words lodged in his

throat. He couldn't remember the last time he had apologized. It might very well have been years. He made decisions with enough forethought and planning that he was almost always right.

He knew he needed to say something. But how many times had he heard his mother apologize to his father? How many times had he heard Daxon take advantage of that apology, use it to twist Marianne to his will and absolve himself of his own actions? Apologies hadn't resolved conflict. They'd been weaponized, used to control.

The door to the helicopter swung open. The pilot snapped to attention. Before Alaric could make the leap of faith and apologize for his heavy-handed behavior, Clara stood and walked down the stairs to the helipad, her bright blue peacoat wrapped tightly around her.

He slammed the lid on his laptop more forcefully than he had intended. Their marriage might be one of necessity, but that didn't mean it had to be like the one he would have had with Celestine. The sooner he remembered that and stopped keeping Clara at arm's length despite pressuring her into marrying him, the sooner they could return to something close to the camaraderie they had achieved in the office. Yes, he needed to maintain awareness, not get drawn too deeply into the emotional aspects of marriage. But he and Clara had succeeded as a team for seven years, including the last year of heightened awareness and tension. They could have that again.

He could start tonight. He had planned on dining alone in the upstairs bedroom he'd had transformed into an office when he'd purchased the house from the royal treasury ten years ago. There was plenty of work to be done, but perhaps he could invite her to work with him, have her review some of the upcoming events that had been planned with the Swiss ambassador and his wife—

His phone rang, cutting off his thoughts. He pulled his cell phone out of his coat pocket and frowned.

"Yes?"

"When were you going to tell me you got married?"

Despite the deep-seated loathing he had for his sire, the weak rasp of Daxon's voice still unnerved him.

"There was no need to inform you at this time."

Daxon's cursing was cut off by a horrific-sounding cough.

"Damn it, Alaric, I'm still king of this country. You are my son and heir."

"Officially, yes. Neither of those roles entitles you to know anything about my personal life."

Something shattered in the background. The weaker Daxon got as the cancer advanced through his body, the more prone he'd become to hurling the nearest object at hand into a wall.

"It does when you follow breaking one of the biggest deals I made for our country by marrying your secretary! Osborne is furious with me!"

"The deal where you bound your son to a girl he'd never met to pay off your debts? Yes, I can see where you might want to ensure the exact details of that stayed quiet."

Up ahead on the snow-covered path, Clara paused, her head slightly cocked to one side. Was she listening to the faint twittering of white-winged larks in the trees nearby? Or could she hear his sordid conversation with his bastard of a father?

"I'm in Switzerland at the moment. We can discuss this later, although there's not much else to be discussed."

Silence descended, an unusual sound when Daxon was around. Then it was broken by a harsh, guttural laughter that made Alaric's skin crawl.

"Briony told me, you know. That you married your secretary."

His fingers tightened around his phone. Briony had become aware all too quickly of Daxon's cruel, selfish nature. Surely she hadn't told him everything. Alaric wouldn't put it past his father to sell the details of Clara's pregnancy to a tabloid to make a fast dollar, especially with his reduced financial circumstances.

"And?"

"I find it rich that my perfect son ended his engagement to one of the wealthiest, most beautiful women in the world to marry a pale, shrewish widow."

Protectiveness reared its head.

"You will not speak of my wife in such a manner. Ever."

"I'm sure you had your reasons. What they are, I'll never understand."

"Nor do you need to. Good night, Your Highness."

"One last thing. I can't help but wonder that my son married a woman from his own office so quickly after ending his engagement of nine years."

The smugness seeping from the phone was enough to make him want to throw the device into the lake.

"What are you implying?"

"Just that you can't have fallen in love in just a few weeks. That's not like you. How long have you and your secretary been screwing?" The damning question was followed by another wheezing laugh. "Guess you're more like me than you thought."

He hung up. Clara turned to look at him, her brow furrowed. He wanted to go to her, to take comfort in the touch of her hand on his shoulder or perhaps even lead her to the master suite, lose himself and his fears in the pleasure of her body.

A want that, if he gave in to, would only prove his father right.

"I have business to attend to." He walked past her. "I'll be in my office until late. The staff will attend to you."

It was better this way, he told himself as he strode through the snow. He had eight months until his son or daughter was born. Perhaps by then, he would have himself under control.

CHAPTER NINE

CLARA WOKE TO weak sunlight filtering in through the curtains. She blinked, confused by the white crown molding and robin's-egg-blue walls, before her mind registered her surroundings. It still took a moment to remember that she was in her husband's vacation home on Lake Geneva.

The husband she hadn't seen since the helicopter had taken off and left her alone with him and a small staff. He'd taken a phone call as they'd exited the aircraft. Daxon, judging by the dark glower on his face by the time he'd hung up. He'd seen her as far as the entry-way before curtly telling her he had business to attend to and would see her at dinner.

That had been two days ago. Aside from the occasional glimpse in the hall, she hadn't seen him at all.

She closed her eyes and sank back into the welcoming embrace of the feather mattress. Alaric had made it clear that there would be no emotional entanglements where she was concerned. She just hadn't expected for him to withdraw from the relationship they'd had as boss and assistant. She'd agreed to marry the man who engaged in conversation with her, who shared his thoughts on improving Linnaea's job market and treated her like she had something intelligent to say.

Was it too much to ask that he extend her the same respect as his wife?

With a frustrated sigh she threw back the cozy blankets and moved to the window. Snowflakes danced against a light gray sky, adding another layer to the white powder already covering the grounds.

She'd spent the first day exploring the house. She'd fallen in love with its unexpectedly cozy charm, from the mahogany wood floors and matching planked ceilings to the massive bay windows in the living room set behind a burgundy couch heaped with pillows and rugs. The living room, kitchen and dining room all had their own fireplaces, as did each of the bedrooms and the library.

The second day she'd returned to the library, browsing through the books before settling on a murder mystery and curling up in an overstuffed chair by the fireplace. Before she'd taken complete leave of her senses and had sex with her boss on top of his desk, she'd spent many nights in her own apartment reading. But in the past month she'd thrown herself even deeper into her work, spreadsheets and schedules keeping her mind off what had transpired between them.

It had been hard to get into the story at first. But gradually she'd relaxed, enjoying the flow of the words and the escalating intensity as the heroine matched wits with a killer hiding in a cast of suspicious characters. Halfway through, as the heroine questioned several suspects, her eyelids had grown unexpectedly heavy. She'd woken nearly two hours later with a blanket draped over her and a fire roaring in the fireplace. Instead of making her feel cared for and cozy, it had enhanced her loneliness.

Which is why, she decided as she turned away from the window, today she would venture out. Getting outside, going into the nearby town she'd spied on their helicopter ride, would raise her spirits. Then tomorrow she would hunt Alaric down and they would have a conversation about her role as princess and queen-to-be. That he thought she would be satisfied with a life of leisure showed how little he really knew her.

Just a good reminder to not romanticize their relationship in any way.

With that empowering thought and a plan in place, she made quick work of getting dressed and went downstairs. A breakfast had been laid out in the kitchen, including an assortment of Swiss cheese tarts and quiches topped with everything from sautéed onion to chopped apples. Enough to feed an army. She wrinkled her nose at the waste. She'd never seen Alaric engage in excess demonstration like this. He wasn't stingy, but he eschewed any useless posturing or grand gestures if they didn't serve a purpose.

She grabbed a good old-fashioned bagel, spread some cream cheese on it and headed for the front door. A walk around the property would do her good. Then she'd visit the servants' quarters and, if the roads were navigable, would have the driver take her into the picturesque town of Rolle.

She was almost to the front door when a board creaked behind her. She turned as Alaric walked down the stairs.

Her heart leaped into her throat. In dark jeans, a navy

sweater with the sleeves pushed up to his elbows and a trace of stubble along his jaw, he looked even more masculine than he usually did in his tailored suits. This Alaric looked rugged, dangerous and all too enticing.

Great job not romanticizing.

"Where are you going?"

"Outside."

He frowned.

"It's cold outside."

She widened her eyes. "What?" She turned and peered out the window. "It snows when it's cold?"

As she turned back, she smacked into a solid wall of muscle. She looked up into narrowed green eyes.

"You're pregnant."

"Yes, pregnant. Not an invalid. I've lived in Linnaea for the past seven years, and I lived in England before that. Plenty of cold winters that I ventured out in."

"Not when you were pregnant."

She wanted to back up, to put physical space between them. Being this close to him, feeling the heat radiate off his muscular frame and the brush of his hard thighs against her legs, made her body respond in ways she didn't want it to. But as soon as she did that, he would have the upper hand.

"Alaric, I've been cooped up in this house for two days. I'm going outside."

She brushed past him and moved to the hall closet. Inside were several new coats, all from brands she knew cost a small fortune. Just like the closet in her room, she thought with a slight sigh as she brushed them aside and pulled out her blue peacoat. She'd brought her own outfits. But Alaric had had someone go shopping for her and stuff the closet in her room with clothes by Versace, Prada and Chanel.

An uncomfortable thought invaded as her hands brushed against the lush velvet of an emerald-colored coat. Miles had done the same thing. At first, she'd accepted his gifts of luxury dresses and expensive jewelry with gratitude, assuming he was showering her with the things he was used to giving. It hadn't been until later when he'd gotten upset at her wearing her old clothes that she realized, too late, the gifts had been his way of molding her into the type of woman he wanted her to be.

Her stomach rolled and she nearly dropped the bagel she still clutched in one hand.

"Then I'm coming with you."

She tugged on her coat, wanting to put as much distance between her and Alaric as possible so she could think. But maybe this was their chance to clear the air. There were so many questions floating around inside her head, so many possibilities of what his sudden change could mean. Unfortunately, without talking to him, she wouldn't find any answers.

"That would be nice."

She looked up to see Alaric blink, the only indicator he was surprised but a gesture she knew very well after working so closely alongside him.

"All right. I'll get my—"

The shrill ring of his phone cut them off. He pulled it out of his pocket and grimaced.

"It's the Swiss ambassador's office."

Her heart sank. She'd spent a year working with Alaric to get the ambassador to agree to an in-person visit to Linnaea to see the country firsthand and all the progress Alaric had made. That the ambassador had finally agreed and come shortly after Alaric's half sister Briony had taken on Linnaea's broken education system had been a stroke of luck that had solidified a new relationship with Switzerland.

It should have been a huge achievement. Instead, it had been overshadowed by their night together and the subsequent weeks of trying to regain her professional foothold. And now…now she had completely been kicked out.

"You should take it. Maybe you could visit with him in person while we're here."

He nodded.

"We'll walk later."

She forced a smile on her face. "Sure."

But she knew later wouldn't come. At least not today. She waited until he was out of sight before she unlocked the front door and walked outside. The cold filled her lungs and gave her a sudden burst of energy, a surprising welcome from the oppressive warmth of the house.

As she walked down the steps and onto the snow-covered circular drive, she let her hand drift down to her belly. She'd only known for a week that she was pregnant. But whenever she thought about the child growing inside her, about holding him or her for the first time in her arms, she knew that no matter what happened with Alaric, she would love this child with every fiber of her being. Her parents had set the example for the kind of mother she wanted to be. If she could be even half the mom her own had been, she would be doing something right.

She'd agreed to marry Alaric because she thought

he'd been serious about his intent to be a better father than his own. And, she acknowledged with a small degree of irritation, he would certainly be a better father than Daxon. He was nothing like his sire, even though she sometimes wondered if he ran such a rigid government because he was trying to stay as far away from the erratic rule his father had imposed for so many years.

The wedding ceremony, the dresses…those small touches had eased so much of her trepidation. She knew Alaric didn't love her. But seeing the evidence of his thoughtfulness, that he had meant what he had said about being involved and making their union a pleasant one for both them and their child, had made her cautiously hopeful.

But now…had she read too much into the wedding? Would he be involved in their marriage and their child the way he'd claimed he'd wanted to be? Or would he get so caught up in work he didn't have time for his child?

"No matter what, baby," she whispered to the tiny life inside her, "I'll be here for you."

CHAPTER TEN

ALARIC GLANCED OUT the window and saw with surprise that the sky had already grown dark. He glanced at his watch and swore. It was just after five o'clock. The conversation with the ambassador had taken nearly two hours, followed by a virtual meeting with one of his economic committees and then another meeting with his new brother-in-law, Cass.

Briony and Cass were honeymooning somewhere in the Maldives for three weeks, but Cass had proven to be invested in Linnaea's financial recovery, both literally and figuratively. His commitment was admirable given that Alaric's father had once kicked Cass and his family out of the country.

Toward the end of their meeting, Briony had appeared onscreen, radiant with a big smile on her face as she'd kissed Cass on the cheek and admonished him for working so late before their dinner reservation. Cass's indulgent grin as he'd told Alaric he'd follow up the next day before exiting out of the meeting had ratcheted up Alaric's guilt to new levels. The former playboy billionaire was making time for his wife and he couldn't even set aside five minutes to walk with his new bride.

After his conversation with Daxon, he'd kept his distance the first couple of days. Daxon's harsh laughter had echoed in his ears every time he'd even thought about Clara. The tiny seed of doubt that had been planted after they'd made love on top of his desk had rooted itself deep in his heart, cunningly winding its way through his veins until it had leaped up and nearly strangled him following the phone call. To look at Clara and think that he had placed her in the same position his father had placed so many women, including Alaric's own mother, had made him so angry at himself he couldn't bear to be around her.

His anger had gradually subsided as he'd focused on work. When he'd gone down to the kitchen to grab a sandwich on the second day, he'd seen the door to the library open and found Clara sleeping in the chair by the fireplace.

Beautiful. That had been his first thought as his eyes had greedily moved over her sleeping form, from the gentle wisps of blond hair escaping from her bun to her dark lashes resting on her pale cheeks. She'd fallen asleep with a book in one hand and her cheek resting in the other. The urge to kneel before her, lean in and gently kiss her awake before scooping her in his arms and taking her back to the master suite had been overwhelming. He'd focused his attention instead on building a fire to ward off the chill seeping through the massive windows overlooking the lake and draping a blanket over her before returning to his office.

Eventually they would introduce physical intimacy into their relationship. He wanted more children. Hopefully she did, too. But when that happened, it needed to be the way his past relationships had been conducted, with a focus solely on physical pleasure. To act when he was feeling this muddled mix of emotions, of anger and guilt and a different type of attraction than what he'd felt for any other woman, was to court chaos.

However, not spending time with his wife was a cowardly move. He'd heard her move around in the adjoining suite that morning and had gone downstairs to join her for breakfast. He hadn't been expecting Clara to agree to his joining her for a walk. And he hadn't missed the disappointment that had flashed in her eyes before she'd withdrawn and told him to take the call.

He'd hesitated, almost invited her to join him…but he hadn't. Daxon's parting words from their last phone conversation had left their mark. It bothered him how much he missed spending time with Clara, her insight and attention to detail. The more he wanted to seek her out, the more he resisted. It had been easier when his engagement to Celestine had kept a barrier between them and he'd been able to just enjoy her company.

Yet by letting Daxon's insults guide his actions, he was giving his father power.

That disquieting thought followed him throughout the house as he searched for his wife. As each room proved to be empty, his frustration turned to concern. Where had she gone?

He pulled out his phone and tried calling her. Concern turned to panic when the call went straight to voice mail. A moment later, he dialed his head of security.

"Yes, Your Highness."

"Where is my wife?"

"She left two hours ago with the driver and Stefan. They went into Rolle."

Clara soaked up the ambience of the little bookstore as she pulled a particularly worn volume off a rickety shelf. The bookstore was in the basement of a restaurant, the worn brick walls and creaky wood floors a haven that had welcomed her with open arms. Even though her designated bodyguard, Stefan, loomed near the doorway, she'd politely but firmly him told not to follow her into the stacks of books.

It would take some getting used to, having a bodyguard shadow her every move when she went out. But for right now, with the low murmur of other customers' voices underlying the soft jazz drifting out from hidden speakers, she could pretend that she was just a normal shopper.

She'd cracked open the book and was scanning the pages when the back of her neck prickled. Pine overrode the scent of old books, wrapping around her with a sensual warmth that let her know exactly who was standing behind her.

"Good evening, Your Highness."

"What are you doing here?"

Alaric's growl made her shiver in a not unpleasant way. Although judging by the thinly veiled anger in his voice, he was not pleased at her trip into town.

"I'm trying to locate my wife, who apparently doesn't understand basic security protocol for members of the royal family."

"Perhaps I would be more familiar if my husband had enough time to say more than 'good morning' to me," she retorted before she could stop herself. If the man wanted to keep her at arm's length, fine, but to keep her prisoner, too? Absolutely not.

Alaric started to say something, but the arrival of a loud tourist group drowned out whatever he was about to say. He grabbed her by the elbow and steered her down the aisle away from the crowd. The narrow shelves zigzagged back and forth in a maze she could have spent hours exploring. Judging by how quickly Alaric was moving, though, she was done exploring for the day.

Claustrophobia pressed in on her. Was this to be her life? Cooped up in the palace or whatever residence they were hiding in, never allowed to go out and do anything resembling a normal life?

They reached the back of the store. Clusters of chairs had been gathered into reading nooks, including several with thick velvet curtains. Alaric guided her into one and undid the gold rope holding the curtains back.

"Do not let anyone within ten feet of us," Alaric barked over her shoulder. She barely caught a glimpse of Stefan turning to stand guard between them and the rest of the bookstore before the curtain fell.

Leaving them in a tight space lit only by the dim glow of a lamp. The intimacy of the space, coupled with the low lighting and the rich, seductive color of the curtains and matching chairs, reminded her of a bordello. It would be all too easy to allow the intimate atmosphere to prompt her into doing something foolish like kissing her husband.

She wrenched her arm free and sat in one of the overstuffed chairs. The more distance between them, the better. Having an attack of hormones was not in her best interest right now.

"I took a guard with me."

"And failed to notify me that you were leaving the house."

Alaric prowled back and forth, his large frame filling up the small space. He reminded her of a caged panther with his dark hair, black V-neck sweater and matching pants. The sleeves had been pushed up to his elbows, revealing his powerful forearms.

"I didn't realize I had to ask permission every time I stepped out the front door."

"You're a princess now, Clara," he snapped. "A future queen, and carrying the heir to the throne. You can't just waltz off anytime you feel like it. Things are different."

"You're right." She stood and poked a finger in his chest. "Things are different. Let's talk about that, shall we? How long are you going to keep shutting me out and treating me like I'm some spoiled princess when I've done nothing but work my tail off to support you and your country?"

He stepped back. She remembered the first time she had seen surprise flash in his green eyes. Her first day on the job when she'd offered a suggestion on an email he'd written, he'd looked thunderstruck, like no one had dared oppose anything he said.

"It was not my intention to shut you out."

"But you have." She wasn't going to let him make excuses. If he had a reason for taking away everything from her and locking her inside a gilded cage, she deserved an explanation. She had gone forward with the marriage in good faith, knowing it was the best decision for her child and for the country even if she'd had valid concerns. And this was how dared to treat her?

"What did I do?" She barely kept her voice steady through her anger and hurt. "I'm not Celestine, Alaric. Stop treating me like her."

His expression darkened, warning flickering across his face as his jaw tightened.

"Don't say that."

"Why not? You are. You've taken away my work, told me to relax, basically clipped my wings and stuffed me into a cage. I don't want to be worthless, Alaric. I want to be a partner. I want to keep doing my job."

"You are not worthless," he ground out.

"Yet you treat me like I'm not good for anything but sitting around and eating fancy treats all day." She cast a glance at the curtain and made a conscious effort to lower her voice. No mean feat when her heart was beating frantically, a headache starting to pound in her temples as she looked ahead to her future and saw nothing but confinement, restriction. "At least when I was your assistant we had tea together and even the occasional meal. Now that we're married, you disappear but seem to expect for me to be ready and waiting whenever you come calling. That's not how this is going to work."

She started to poke him again for emphasis, but he caught her wrist in his grasp.

"Don't tell me how things are going to go, Clara. I've always called the shots. Us getting married hasn't changed that."

"Then it seems I've made a mistake."

He froze. "What do you mean?"

"I'm not going to be a prisoner, Alaric. If our honeymoon means I'm going to be stranded in that house by myself for the next two weeks, I'm flying back to Linnaea tomorrow."

She started to pivot away. With a gentle tug he turned her back to him, slid an arm around her waist and pinioned her against his chest.

"Don't leave."

Words of protest rose to her lips. But beneath her anger, her brain picked up the slight hint of apology in his voice.

"Why not?"

He let out a deep sigh.

"I've never been a husband before. When I was engaged to Celestine, she made it perfectly clear in her communications to me what she expected of our relationship. She was to be taken care of financially and, as long as she conducted herself with discretion, would be allowed to do whatever she wanted. In her mind, I owed her since my father essentially bought her and her fortune. Guilt guided my actions."

Her past slammed into her present with sickening clarity. Miles had bought himself a trophy wife. Alaric had snagged himself a future queen. *No, Daxon was behind the contract,* she amended. Alaric was placing too much blame on himself for the arrangement with Celestine. But he had let it continue, even as he'd grown and matured. And now he'd entered into yet another contract with another fiancée he'd purchased, not for her wealth but for the child she carried. Worse still, he was treating her like she was his former fiancée and not the woman he'd been working alongside for the past seven years. That he had so quickly put her into the same box as Celestine, a woman who had seemed to glory in creating as much drama for Alaric as possible, made her chest tighten in pain and shame.

She'd made the same mistake. Again.

She tried to pull away. Alaric kept a firm grip on her waist.

"But you're right."

She leaned back and frowned.

"Are you ill?"

"Not to my knowledge. Why?"

"I think I can count on one hand the number of times you've told me I was right."

His chest rumbled against hers as he chuckled. "I'll mark it on my calendar. It will take me a while to learn how to navigate being both a leader and a husband. You've been a crucial part of this administration, Clara, and I don't intend for you to sit on a couch the rest of your life eating chocolates. I want you to be involved in Linnaea's future."

Ridiculous how such a non-sentimental statement could warm her.

"Well…thank you."

With her anger slowly subsiding, she became acutely aware of just how tightly they were melded together. The last time Alaric had held her this close, the muscles of his arm pressed against her back, she'd been arching against the thrusts of his body as he'd wrapped his fingers in her hair and kissed her senseless. The heat in her veins turned from a fiery burst of anger to a languid, seductive song that made her relax against him.

A growing hardness against her thigh signaled that she wasn't the only one being affected by their surroundings.

Slowly, she looked up. Alaric was staring down at her, his eyes glittering with intensity.

Just like the first, and only, time they'd kissed, she wasn't sure who moved first. Their lips met, one hand pressing against her back and the other sliding down to the curve of her hip, fingers urging her closer until she was straddling his thigh. She clung to his shoulders and sighed, opening her mouth to him. He growled and pressed deeper, his tongue sweeping across her lower lip before he claimed her in an intimate dance that made her heavy with desire.

When they'd kissed in his office, they'd moved at a frenetic pace that had left her breathless. They'd gone from a frantic kiss to him lifting her onto his desk, sliding her skirt up and trailing his fingers over the sensitive skin of her thighs. The moment he'd realized she hadn't been wearing panties beneath the tight evening gown, he'd shuddered and asked if she wanted this. She'd kissed him for an answer as her fingers had undone his zipper before wrapping around his impressive length. It had been incredible, but far too short.

Now, even though the world was just beyond the curtain and waited for them with all of its messiness, now they had a little time.

Her hands moved up to his hair, her fingers tangling in the thick, silky strands. She savored the texture, dropped one hand down to his neck and thrilled at the cords of muscle tight beneath his skin. As her fingertips grazed over his throat, he suddenly slid both hands under her thighs, lifted her up and spun around. Gently, he set her down on one of the chairs, his lips never leaving hers, as his hands drifted down to the hem of her shirt.

"Alaric…"

He froze. And then he was gone, releasing her so quickly she fell back into against the chair.

Alaric moved as far away as he could to the curtain, his chest rising and falling as his harsh breathing filled the small space.

"Clara… I'm sorry."

"Why?" She stood, reached out to him, tried not to let her hurt show when he jerked away from her touch. Three days ago she hadn't been sure she was ready for the physical intimacies Alaric had hinted would come in time with their marriage. But now, after being reminded of just how truly good they were together, she wanted nothing more than to feel his body against hers again. To feel beautiful and sexy and alive. "We're married now, Alaric."

"I'm a prince. You're a princess. We're next in line to the throne." He gestured to the close confines of the reading nook. "This is beyond inappropriate. If we were to get caught, the media would rain hell on us. It's taken me years to build Linnaea's reputation back up, despite Daxon's and Celestine's efforts to ruin it. I don't want to risk that again."

Mortification stung her cheeks. She'd been concerned that Alaric had placed her in the same category as his ex-fiancée. But could she blame him when she'd ground her hips against his thigh with people just steps away, the same way Celestine had been plastered between those two men at the dance club in New York?

"I'm sorry, Alaric."

"It's my fault, Clara. I brought you back here."

Exhaustion settled into her bones and threatened to drag her down.

"We both made a mistake."

He stirred. "Clara, I don't think—"

"Could we discuss this later in a more private setting?" She nodded toward the curtain. "We've risked enough for tonight."

His mouth thinned into a grim line. He nodded and held back the curtain.

"Go. I'll wait a few minutes for you and Stefan to leave. I'll see you at the house."

She walked past him, keeping as much distance between them as possible. Thankfully there were no customers in sight, no one except Stefan, who stood ten feet away, his eyes scanning the shelves. When he saw her walking toward him, he all but snapped to attention.

"Ready to go, Your Highness?"

"Yes. I'm sorry if I got you in trouble, Stefan."

Stefan blinked in surprise, then bowed his head. "The prince was displeased, but he corrected me on protocol for future outings."

What future outings? she thought glumly as Stefan escorted her to the car waiting outside. It looked like, at least for the foreseeable future, she was truly going to be trapped at the lake house, just like Miles had confined her to the penthouse. After the incident in the reading nook, Alaric would probably disappear into his office for the rest of their honeymoon. And unlike her first marriage, where she'd stayed primarily out of fear and loneliness, now she had to stay for the sake of her unborn child.

At least she'd had eight years of freedom. She had just never pictured trading one cage for another.

CHAPTER ELEVEN

ALARIC HEARD HER before she walked into the kitchen. The soft padding of her footsteps on the wood floor, a gentle melody as she hummed a song. The domestic sounds calmed the heightened state of awareness he'd been in since last night.

Last night when he'd almost taken his wife for the second time in a very inappropriate place that could have caused a disaster.

What was wrong with him? He'd always conducted his previous affairs with the utmost care—faraway cities, upscale hotels that catered to elite clientele and operated with the highest discretion. His previous lovers had been enjoyable. But with Clara…once he'd tasted her, felt the delicious heat of her body and seen her come alive for him, she had become a drug he couldn't get enough of.

Worry slithered into his thoughts, the same worry that had been steadily growing ever since that night. If he was willing to risk everything he'd worked so hard for, everything the people of his country deserved, for a moment of passion, was he fit to lead? Or was he too much like Daxon at his core to be a good representative of the Linnaean people? He'd prided himself on his ability to remain in control. But perhaps it was because he hadn't been faced with the right kind of temptation until now.

A temptation he had married and was expecting a child with. It wasn't Clara's fault that he behaved like that around her. But it was something he needed to regain control of. Fast. Avoiding Clara would only work for so long. They were married. The news would come out in time. Time to take control of the narrative.

Clara rounded the corner, her eyes focused on a book. Her blond hair had been gathered into a loose bun on top of her head, long strands already falling out to grace the back of her neck and frame her delicate face. Beneath an ivory cardigan she wore pale pink lounge pants and a matching top that clung to the curves of her breasts. Her nipples were pebbled beneath the thin material. His entire body tightened.

Stay focused.

Clara's head suddenly snapped up and her eyes widened as she took in Alaric standing by the kitchen sink.

"What are you doing here?"

"Good morning to you, too."

Her cheeks darkened to a rosy color. "Sorry. Um, good morning. Everything all right?"

"Yes. Why wouldn't it be?"

"It's just… I haven't seen you down here for breakfast since we arrived. I wasn't sure if someone saw…" Her blush deepened. "That is, if something made its way into the news…"

"No." He waved her worry aside. "Nothing like that. Can I get you something to eat?"

She blinked in surprise. "Um… I can get it myself."

"Clara, you're my wife. You're pregnant. And I've left you alone for three days on our honeymoon. I'm making you breakfast."

At last, she nodded.

"That would be nice. Tea and toast, please."

He arched a brow. "Aren't you supposed to be eating for two?"

She grimaced. "Hard to do when I wake up every morning feeling like I've just gotten off a boat in a thunderstorm. I'll eat more later."

He wanted to push, but judging by the queasy look on her face when she glanced at his half-eaten bagel covered in a liberal amount of cream cheese and piled with smoked salmon and cucumber, pushing would result in a very unpleasant morning.

He moved around the kitchen, the silence broken by the occasional clink of the teacup or the whisper as Clara turned a page in her book. It was, he realized with some surprise, a pleasant silence, one he didn't feel the need to fill with inane chatter. The last time he'd taken a lover to dinner—over two years ago—she hadn't stopped talking, from the time he'd picked her up at her hotel in Paris until he'd dropped her off after a theater performance. She'd coyly invited him up to her room, but he hadn't been able to muster even the faintest desire to join her in her bed.

He hadn't been with anyone since. Truthfully, even though he'd told himself it was his upcoming marriage to Celestine that had led to his streak of celibacy, he'd grown tired of the brief flings, the businesslike arrangement of his sexual encounters, the lack of a connection beyond mutual physical pleasure. Pleasure that had dulled over the years, each encounter bleeding into the next.

There had been, too, a dull throb that had grown into an ache with each rendezvous. He'd always held a part of himself back from his previous lovers, knowing nothing would come of their time together. Perhaps that was why he'd sought out the women he had: emotionally distant, independently wealthy, few mutual interests that would spark something beyond a pleasantly shared meal and good sex.

There hadn't been a single woman he'd been with over the years who would be like Clara was now: content to spend a few minutes in silence reading as he made her breakfast.

This was more what he had envisioned when he had proposed to Clara, this satisfying coexistence.

He set a plate with lightly buttered toast and a teacup in front of her.

"Thank you," she said with a smile as if he'd just given her a diamond bracelet.

That was one of the things he'd always liked about Clara, he reflected as he sat across from her. Despite her reputation for being his hard-nosed executive assistant, she could also be one of the most relaxed, easygoing people he'd ever met.

Which made his treatment of her the last few days even more unacceptable.

"What would you think about having dinner tonight?"

She looked up. "Dinner?"

"Yes."

A frown creased her brow. "Breakfast and dinner in one day. Why do I feel like you're about to tell me something bad?"

He chuckled. "Nothing so sinister. You were right. I've overreacted. While there will be more regulations on travel, I can't keep you locked in the house."

One dark blond brow arched up as her lips twisted into a sardonic smile that made his blood stir.

"Glad to know we're on the same page."

"It won't be the same as it was when you were my secretary."

"Executive assistant."

He bit back a grin.

"Yes, assistant. But, Clara, I do need to know when you're going to be gone. It's not some obsessive need to control you. The world is more dangerous for members of a royal family. Even though the majority of our country and Switzerland support the treaty, there are those who are vehemently opposed. I have to keep you and our child safe."

She looked down at her toast for a moment before finally nodding. "I understand. I don't like it, but I understand."

"I know it's not what you probably envisioned when you married me."

"I never envisioned marrying you at all." A slight grin softened the sting of her words, although it disappeared quickly as her expression darkened. "It's just… I haven't told you much about my marriage to Miles."

Just hearing the man's name sent an unexpected bolt of jealousy through him.

"No, you haven't."

"I hinted that it was not a pleasant marriage." She pulled the tea bag out of her cup and watched it twirl back and forth, drops of amber liquid falling onto her plate. "He became very controlling. He didn't like me leaving his apartment in London without him or his mother accompanying me to wherever I was going. His mother picked out what I wore, took me to her hair stylist." She set the tea bag down and stared at the steam rising off the surface. "I wasn't my own person anymore."

Anger churned in his gut, along with the familiar uncomfortableness of guilt. Anger that Miles and his abominable-sounding mother had treated Clara so horribly, and guilt that, while not as extreme, he had been pushing Clara in a similar manner with his restrictions and lack of attention. He'd taken away her job, something she'd been very good at, because he had been uncertain of how he would feel working so closely with her now that their roles had changed. Not because it was the best thing for Clara or for Linnaea, but because of his own discomfort.

She looked up with a small smile. "When you told me I had to ask you about where I was going, I panicked. I was afraid I was falling back into a similar place I had been with Miles. But I understand the difference, the issue of security."

If he'd thought he couldn't feel any more guilty, her understanding only added to the weight pressing on his shoulders.

"I appreciate that, Clara. But I should have talked with you before issuing commands. We worked well together before this change in our relationship, and I should have trusted you by talking to you."

She paused for a moment before nodding once. "Thank you, Alaric."

"There's nothing to thank me for. I didn't handle this well. Which is why I have two proposals."

A teasing light made her blue eyes sparkle. "The last proposal you made was certainly interesting."

"Nothing so drastic this time. The first is that I'd like for you to work with me today. I could use your insight on some of the communications going to the ambassador's staff and a meeting we're setting up next month with the president of the Swiss Confederation."

Her shoulders sagged in relief. "That sounds nice. I never thought I'd miss work so much." She tapped a finger on her book. "I've enjoyed reading, but this is much more time than I'm used to."

"Which brings me to my second point. Would you like to have dinner with me tonight? There's a restaurant just outside of Rolle."

"Are you comfortable with going out and being seen by the public?"

"It's something that needs to happen. I think it would be good for both of us to get out of the house, too, and see some of the local sights. Isn't that what a honeymoon is for?"

The local sight Alaric had picked for their dinner proved to be one of the most exclusive restaurants on the shores of Lake Geneva. Perched on a blufftop that overlooked the lake, the main dining room was dotted with intimate tables and flickering candles. A stone fireplace dominated one side of the room, while the other three featured floor-to-ceiling windows with incredible views of the countryside. Their waiter guided them around the perimeter to a private room tucked off to the side, complete with its own small fireplace and a table set for two. A vase with a red rose stood in stark relief against the white tablecloth, two small tealights flickering on either side of the vase.

Clara tried to ignore the whispers she heard behind them as the waiter pulled out her chair. When she glanced at the dining room, it was to see numerous heads whipping around in a fatal attempt not to be caught starting.

"I'm guessing we'll be featured on the morning news."

Alaric glanced at the curious diners and shrugged. "It was time. I had our public relations office send out a press release tonight anyway."

"You what?"

He looked up at her, his brows drawing together in a frown. "I'd asked you earlier about sharing our pictures from the wedding."

He had, she acknowledged. But she hadn't expected a full media campaign.

"I thought that would be something we'd do together."

"It's not like a standard civilian marriage, Clara. Anything that goes public like that has to go through our PR department."

She knew that. Of course she knew that. Since the department had been formed a couple months ago, she'd sent over numerous articles and sound bites for them to put together into a story or for sharing the palace's social media. But being restricted herself was going to take some getting used to.

Part of her wanted to fold in on herself, the way she used to with Miles. It had been a habit she'd developed when they'd dated. Whenever he would shoot her down, she'd agree and withdraw. It avoided conflict and kept things at least manageable between the two of them. After her marriage, she'd swung the other direction, standing firm in almost every situation and not budging an inch. It had helped her on numerous occasions. But it had also kept people at arm's length. It hadn't been until she'd grown closer to Meira and started talking more with Briony that she'd realized just how much she'd used her supposed spine of steel to keep herself safe.

There had to be a compromise between the two parts of herself.

"Could I be involved in decisions like that?"

Alaric looked up from the menu in surprise. "What?"

"I understand the need to follow protocol," she said, her words tumbling over each other as nerves got the better of her. "I've lived it for seven years. I've enforced it more times than I can count. But I'd like to feel like a partner in this relationship as much as possible. Even just being told what's going to happen, instead of being told after the fact, would make me feel like I'm respected and not just an ornamental chess piece being moved around the board."

Alaric stared at her for a long moment, his eyes narrowed in thought. Part of her felt like she'd overstepped. But the other part, the part that had gone toe to toe with His Royal Highness, struggled to not say more and push her case.

Alaric surprised her by reaching across the table and grabbing her hand in a light grasp.

"A reasonable request. I will most likely need to be reminded from time to time."

She squeezed his fingers before letting go of his hand and picking up her own menu. "Thank you, Alaric."

The rest of the evening passed in a very pleasant fashion. Their waiter brought them dishes like Swiss onion soup, saffron risotto with creamy baked mushrooms and *Zurcher Pfarrhaustorte*, a tart stuffed with grated apples, toasted nuts and cinnamon and baked to perfection. For the first time since she'd known Alaric, their conversation didn't revolve around political deals or meetings or upcoming legislation. She told him about her parents, from reading in the corner of her father's mechanic shop while he worked on cars to summers spent at the beach with both of her parents. He surprised her by sharing memories of his mother and growing up in the palace, including one time when his mother had taught him how to slide down the banister in the main hall and he'd nearly taken out a visiting dignitary.

"She sounds like a wonderful mother," Clara said with a laugh.

"She was." Alaric's expression darkened slightly. "She was taken too soon."

Clara looked down at her half-eaten tart. She knew that the queen had passed away quickly and unexpectedly of a heart attack years ago. Judging by the look on Alaric's face, though, there was more to the story.

There always was.

She glanced toward the dining room again. Would Temperance and Stanley see the press release about her marriage? Would they connect the dots, that their former daughter-in-law had married the future king of

Linnaea? They lived in Los Angeles now, a world away from Eastern Europe. But technology had connected the farthest corners of the earth. As much as she wanted to believe there was a chance they'd miss it, she imagined it was only a matter of time.

The real question was, what would they do when they found out? Would they leave her alone, as they had these past eight years? Or would they try to seek revenge, angry that their former daughter-in-law was trying to move on with her life?

She yanked herself out of the past. Alaric had just confided something intensely personal and here she was thinking about herself.

"Losing a mother is never easy." She glanced down at her stomach. "If…if it's a girl, we could name her Marianne. In honor of her."

The smile that broke across Alaric's face warmed her from head to toe. She'd never seen such joy on his face.

"I would like that, Clara. Very much. Unless you'd prefer to name her after your mother?"

"We could use her name as a middle name. It would work perfectly, actually. Rose."

"Princess Marianne Rose Van Ambrose. It is perfect." He cocked his head to one side. "You don't speak much about your parents."

Her chest tightened.

"It's hard to," she finally said. "They were…" She smiled even as she barely spoke past the lump in her throat. "They were wonderful."

Alaric reached across the table and threaded his fingers through hers in a gesture that, judging by his rapid blinking, surprised both of them. Slowly, she curled her own hand around his.

"They were older. My father contracted cancer. It ran in his family. He died when I was a teenager. And then my mom…" She focused her gaze on her plate. "It seems so stupid. Pneumonia. Something you hear about all the time but you think there's no way it could happen to your family. And then it does and you're alone and then you make foolish decisions."

Alaric's grip tightened on hers.

"Your marriage to Miles."

She nodded, surprised by how easily the words suddenly came. It had taken several glasses of wine to get to the point of confiding in Meira last summer. But somehow, sitting in the restaurant with Alaric holding her hand, she felt safe.

"I was lonely. Young. I didn't know hardly anyone in London. I mistook distraction from my grief for something more."

"Judging by the self-loathing in your voice, it's something you still haven't forgiven yourself for."

Her head snapped up. He stared at her, his gaze intense but kind.

"Not completely, no. It's hard to trust yourself or others after making such a big mistake."

Alaric's chuckle held a note of sadness. "I understand. I said something similar to Cass, actually, when he nearly torpedoed his relationship with my sister."

She laughed. "You gave Prince Cassius Adama relationship advice?"

"I did. And he took it."

"What did you say?"

The mirth disappeared from Alaric's face, replaced

by a distant thoughtfulness. His thumb started to trace lazy circles on the back of her hand. Each subsequent stroke upped the heat slowly building inside her. Such a simple touch, but it made her feel cared for.

"That he was making decisions based on horrible examples he'd seen of relationships. That it was easier for him to stay withdrawn because getting involved was too scary."

Her mouth dropped open.

"That's…very insightful."

And almost frightening. He could have been describing her. Or, she realized with a start, himself. His parents' marriage, and his father's numerous affairs, were hardly sterling examples of love.

She gazed at him, her eyes running over the sharp planes of his face, his full lips relaxed into a slight smile. He'd smiled more in the last hour than he had in the past year. He hadn't judged her for her hasty decisions.

She swallowed hard. Suddenly she wanted to tell him everything, to have him see her fully as no other person had.

He squeezed her hand again before he released it. The loss of his touch robbed her of her moment of confidence.

"Tell me more about your parents. It sounds like you at least had a positive example of a marriage."

She shoved her negative musings away and obliged his request, reminiscing about collecting shells and picnicking on the sand on a checkered blanket her mother had sewn. By the time Alaric escorted her out to the car, her good mood was restored.

Alaric sat across from her as he had on the ride in.

She looked out the window as their driver navigated out of town. A few lights sparkled here and there in the windows of the elegant homes scattered along the water's edge. The pleasant hum of the car's engine, the dark interior and the heated leather seats made her drowsy.

I'll just close my eyes for a moment.

"Clara?"

A voice seemed to come from far away, a deep voice that wrapped her in a pleasant warmth.

"Mmm?"

"We're home."

"Mmm."

She didn't want to open her eyes, didn't want to get up. This was the most relaxed she'd felt in days.

A sensation that promptly disappeared when an arm slid under her legs and another slid around her back. Her eyes flew open as Alaric hauled her into his arms and got out of the car.

"Alaric, what are you doing?"

"Carrying you inside." He nodded to the driver, who was watching them with a smile on his face. "Good night, Frederick."

"Your Highness."

She buried her face in Alaric's coat.

"I'm mortified."

"Why?"

"You're carrying me like I'm a child."

"No, I'm carrying the woman who's carrying my child."

She thought he would set her down on the front porch. But he continued inside, up the stairs and down the hall as if she weighed nothing more than a piece of paper. Another unexpected moment that, like the sweet additions to their wedding, wound its way through her body and wrapped around her heart. Slowly, she allowed herself to relax in his arms, to savor the strength of his grasp.

It would be so easy to get used to being treated like this. So easy to let herself open up to a man who made her feel treasured with his surprisingly romantic gestures.

Finally, they reached her door.

"You can set me down now."

He opened the door and stepped inside. The room, which had felt as large as her apartment at the palace, seemed to shrink as he walked to the bed and gently laid her down.

"Good night, Clara."

He started to pull away, but she kept her arms looped around his neck. Whether it was the incredible food or the enjoyable conversation or her self-reflection at dinner, she couldn't say. But something emboldened her to lean up and press her lips against Alaric's.

"Thank you for a wonderful evening," she whispered as she started to pull away.

Alaric's hands slid into her hair and slowly tugged her back against him. He sat on the edge of the bed as he deepened their kiss, his lips firm against hers. Without the franticness of the first time they'd kissed, or the threat of discovery and the tension from their argument that had hovered over them the second time, there was nothing but a sense of delicious freedom and wantonness as she leaned into him.

She had intended to only kiss him. But when his

fingers crept beneath the collar of her coat and pushed the fabric off her shoulders, she sucked in a shuddering breath. Was she ready for this? Could she sleep with her husband knowing that it wouldn't lead to anything more than the pleasant camaraderie they already shared?

His fingers slid under the strap of her dress, sending a shiver across her skin. He slowly continued to pull the dress down until she was bare from the waist up, sitting on her bed in a puddle of black satin. She opened her eyes as Alaric pulled back, his gaze shimmering with emerald fire as he grasped her hands in his and held her arms out away from her body. Her first instinct was to cover herself as her old insecurities rose up. He'd never seen her nude. What if he didn't like what he saw?

"You're beautiful, Clara." He released one of her hands to cup her breast, the soft touch sending heat spiraling through her veins. "So beautiful."

Her doubts fled. Only desire remained as she lay back on the bed.

"Make love to me, Alaric."

CHAPTER TWELVE

ALARIC STARED AT HER. For one frightening moment, there was nothing but silence.

And then his gaze moved down her body. His eyes glowed molten green as he caressed her naked body, each lingering look more intimate and scorching than the last. She reached down, sucked in a deep breath, and slowly pushed the rest of her dress off, including the silk panties that had clung to her hips like a second skin.

He didn't move, didn't flinch, just watched as she undressed for him. She felt wonderfully brazen, wanton and seductive, her hands gliding down her own body and back up as she slipped off her shoes and lay back once more against the pillows.

He took one step forward. She pushed herself up onto her elbows, her eyes drifting down to his hips. Any lingering doubts were banished by the hard evidence between his thighs. Despite her lying naked before him, a blush stole over her cheeks.

"I don't think our current situation is fair."

Was that her voice? Husky, low, seductive?

A wicked grin she would never have imagined Alaric

was capable of if she hadn't seen it crept over his handsome face and made her belly tighten.

"What are you going to do about it?"

The challenge reverberated through her. She paused, self-doubt creeping in. Their first time, their only time, had been when he'd been raw and hurting. What if their explosive chemistry had been the result of a moment in time? She'd only been with Miles. She wasn't experienced like she assumed Alaric's previous lovers had been.

Stop.

A tiny voice whispered the command in her ear. She listened, steadied her breathing and let herself relax, focused on the warmth of desire that had been building since he'd carried her inside the house. Her fears melted away as she slowly stood and crossed to him. When she pulled the hem of his shirt from his pants, her fingers grazing the chiseled muscles of his abdomen, he hissed.

"Taking your time?"

His growl rippled over her, emboldened her as she slowly undid his buttons.

"We didn't get much time in your office." She leaned down and placed a kiss to his bared chest. His body went rigid beneath her touch. "Now would seem an appropriate moment to go slow."

He stood still as she undid his tie, slid his shirt and suit jacket from his shoulders. He tensed but didn't stop her as she unbuckled his belt. She hooked her fingers in the waistband of his pants and boxers and slowly eased them down over his muscular thighs, the low rumbling sound in his throat sending an electrifying thrill through her.

When her fingers grazed his impressive length and she felt him swell even more against the slightest touch, an urge seized her. She sank to her knees.

"Clara, you don't have to…"

His words trailed off and ended in a guttural moan as she wrapped one hand around the base of his hardness and took him in her mouth. She loved the way his hips arched forward, his hands tangling in her hair as he groaned her name. When she looked up, it was to see him with his head thrown back, his jaw taut. He looked powerful, strong and on the verge of losing control.

Because of her. Because of how she touched him.

That carnal knowledge spurred her on as she cupped him, savored the ever-increasing hardness of his body.

"Clara."

He bit her name out. Strong hands reached down and hauled her to her feet, pressing her body against his, naked skin to naked skin. Her lips parted on a gasp just as he kissed her, his tongue sweeping into her mouth as he laid claim to her.

"Fair is fair, wife."

Before she could blink, he swept her into his arms and deposited her on the bed. He shed the rest of his clothes before joining her, caging her beneath his body. She started to part her legs. He kissed her again, swiftly, and then pulled back with a chuckle.

"Not yet."

He trailed his lips down her neck to her breasts, circling one globe and then the other with the tip of his tongue before capturing each peak in his mouth and sucking with long, drawn-out movements that made her writhe beneath him as her fingers tangled in his hair. He continued his sensual onslaught, moving down over her belly, her hips, until he paused just above her most sensitive skin.

Her thighs pressed together of their own accord. The few times she and Miles had had sex, it had been fleeting, a few thrusts for his own pleasure and then it was over. She'd never experienced a man touching her the way Alaric was touching her now.

He pressed a kiss to her core, an open-mouthed caress that made her body curve up into his touch before she could stop herself.

"Alaric."

He parted her legs, and she let him. How could she stop him when he looked at her with gleaming eyes filled with male satisfaction and appreciation? Appreciation for *her* body. When he leaned down and his tongue danced over her skin, she cried out, asking him, begging him as the tension built inside her, wound her so tight as pleasure spiraled from his touch throughout her body.

Just as she felt herself on the edge of finally achieving release, he pulled back with a dark chuckle.

"Alaric!" she cried out, her hands reaching for him. "That's not—"

He moved up her body with lightning speed and pinned her to the mattress with his weight, one hand forming to the curve of her hip as the other smoothed the hair back from her forehead. He stared at her for a moment, as if seeing her for the first time, some unknown emotion glittering in the green depths.

"I want to be inside you this first time."

She blinked back the sudden hot tears at his words. "I don't know if you remember, but we already did this once," she said with a cheeky smile to cover her emotional response.

"Our first time as husband and wife."

What did one say to such an unexpected and tender sentiment? He gave her little time to ponder the question as he pressed the tip of his hardness against her and robbed her of her voice. Slowly, he slid inside her, her body stretching to accommodate him, her hips cradling his thighs until he filled her.

He kissed her once more, soft and gentle, before he began to move with long, slow thrusts. She met every stroke, her hands caressing his back, her fingers gliding over his face as she kissed his jaw, his cheek, his nose, his lips.

The crescendo built inside her once more, taking her higher with every touch.

"Alaric..."

"Clara."

She burst into a thousand pieces, riding a wave of pleasure so intense she swore she saw stars. Her nails raked down his back, and he followed a moment later, burying his face against her shoulder as he shuddered in her arms.

He relaxed against her, the weight of his body keeping her pinned in place. She sighed as her fingers drifted languidly over his back, his shoulders, his neck, his skin covered in a fine sheen of sweat.

"I like slow."

His words teased a chuckle out of her.

"Me, too."

He lifted his head and shot her the most carefree, relaxed smile she'd ever seen.

One that faded a moment later as he glanced at the clock.

"It's getting late."

"So?"

He started to push up. "I should go." He waved his hand at the bed. "I don't…that is…"

She forced a smile to her face. "I understand. This was…nice."

He arched a brow. "Nice?"

"Okay, very nice."

He eased himself back down. "I don't know how to be a husband, Clara."

"I can't say I have that much experience being a wife." She gestured toward the door. "You were up-front with me, Alaric. I know what to expect and what not to. If staying here crosses a boundary for you, I don't want you to feel like you have to stay."

Even though I really want you to.

Miles had always kept a separate bed in his own master suite. She'd never woken up next to him. Not that she'd ever wanted to, not when she didn't know if she'd wake up in bed with the charmer or an abusive drunk.

But with Alaric…

She gave herself a slight shake. He wasn't comfortable. No point in entertaining what-ifs.

A frown darkened his face.

"It's not…" He glanced around the bed. "How about I lie here with you? Just for a bit?"

"Alaric, I'm a big girl. You don't—"

Before she could finish her sentence, he rolled to the side, slid an arm beneath her waist and pulled her against his chest. Even though they'd just made love, the intimacy of being pressed against him sent a languid wave of heat through her body.

She waited for a moment, then slowly let herself relax, her head dropping onto his shoulder as she shyly rested one hand on his chest.

"Just for a bit," she murmured as her eyes slowly closed.

It was still dark when Alaric awoke. Clara's breath feathered across his chest, her head resting just above his heart, one hand curled against his skin. He gave in to his first inclination, to gently trace his fingers up and down her back and kiss the top of her silken head. She murmured in her sleep and curled deeper into his embrace.

He had never fallen asleep with any of his past lovers, much less woken up in their bed. It was an intimacy he didn't entertain. With the clock ticking on his upcoming marriage to Celestine, there had been no point in risking a woman developing any affection for him. More complications and messy tabloid coverage had been the last thing he'd needed.

But, he realized as his fingers trailed down Clara's spine, over the curve of her hip, lingered on the slight swelling of her belly, he had missed out on something truly incredible in doing so.

He wasn't so blind to emotions that he had missed the disappointment in Clara's eyes when he'd started to leave, nor her attempts at insisting she was fine if he didn't stay. The part he hadn't shared, that had made him start to leave in the first place, was that he had wanted to stay. No woman had ever made him want to stay.

Until Clara.

He hadn't planned on falling asleep with her. But as he'd lain there in the dark, as she'd slowly relaxed against him and slipped into slumber in the circle of his arms, he hadn't wanted to disturb her. He'd told himself he would just rest his eyes.

And now here he was, in his wife's bed, not wanting to be anywhere else. Being at the lake house with her, without the busyness of the palace, the constant meetings and without his forced engagement hanging over his head, made him even more aware of the traits he liked about his wife. Her kindness, her support, her acceptance of him. Her argument, too, that she be allowed to resume her roles, had induced simultaneous feelings of guilt and an admiration made all the more potent by the tenderness creeping in with every moment spent in her presence. One of his chief regrets about Celestine had been how little she had cared about Linnaea. She had ignored or flat-out refused to attend any of the special events he'd invited her to, the last being the art museum opening in Eira in the fall.

Clara stirred in his arms, her fingernails grazing his chest and reigniting the spark of desire that had blazed into an inferno so intense he'd barely been able to breathe past his desire when she'd lain back on the bed and asked him to make love to her. He had an incredible wife who shared his passion for his country, who wanted to be involved, who was carrying his child.

Was it too much to hope that, at last, everything in his life was finally on the right track?

His hand drifted back up and grazed the underside of her breast. A soft moan escaped her lips. His fingers quested higher, drifted over a pebbled nipple with the lightest caress. Clara's eyes fluttered open as a slow smile spread across her face.

"Alaric?"

He gently rolled her onto her back, pinning her hips with his. She gasped and squirmed against his growing hardness. He reached up, grasped her wrists in one hand and held them above her head.

"Not fair," she laughed up at him.

"Perhaps this will be more to your liking."

He leaned down and captured one nipple in her mouth, grazing his teeth over the sensitive bud. She arched up into his touch and moaned his name. The sound of her voice stripped away any semblance of restraint. His other hand drifted down to the wetness between her thighs. He stroked her skin, slid one finger, then two, into her wet heat, nearly came undone when she clenched around him.

"Alaric, please!"

He nudged her thighs apart and slid inside, shuddering as she surrounded him, her bare breasts pressing against his chest while he continued to hold her hands captive above her head. Each stroke was just a bit harder, his rhythm quickening as his pleasure and desire soared to a fever pitch.

She cried out, coming undone once more. He followed a moment later. Molten heat flooded his veins. He released her wrists, meeting her halfway as their arms flew around each other, their lips pressed together until he couldn't tell where he ended and she began.

CHAPTER THIRTEEN

CLARA FOCUSED ON the screen of the laptop Alaric had procured for her, the words blurring. She'd reread the email she didn't know how many times. She cast a glance at the door he'd disappeared out of to take a call. Alaric's ringing phone had startled them both out of a deep sleep just after dawn. For a moment, she'd been too content wrapped up in the warmth of his arms and snuggled against his naked body to pay much attention. But when the unknown caller had called again, Alaric had answered with barely concealed irritation that had quickly turned to brusque concern. Daxon had taken a turn for the worse early that morning. The doctors said he was stable for now, but they'd reduced his time from a year down to just a few months at best.

As much pain as Daxon had caused, Clara hadn't missed the worry on Alaric's face as he'd spoken with the palace physician.

Finally, she slammed her computer shut. She needed to get up and move around, refocus before she did any more work. Selfish as it was, it wasn't just her concern for Alaric and Daxon.

No, after the physical and emotional closeness of

yesterday, it was hard to keep the feelings that had been growing for the past year at bay. From making her breakfast and listening to her past to his happiness at her name suggestion for the baby and the incredible intimacy they'd shared last night, she was struggling to not let her emotions have free rein.

What, she asked herself for the hundredth time in the past twenty-four hours, was she feeling for her husband? Was it a naturally developing affection for her new partner? Or was it something more?

She heaved a frustrated sigh and headed for the door. She stepped out into the hall just as Alaric walked around the corner, one hand wrapped around his phone, the other curled into a fist.

"What happened?"

He shook his head.

"The old man's a damned fool. He's refusing most recommendations. Said he knows the end is near and he's going to live it on his terms, not some damned doctor's."

She reached out slowly and laid a tentative hand on his arm. When he didn't pull away, she moved closer and moved her hand to his back, rubbing gently at the tension knotting his muscles.

"I was about to go on a walk, get out and move a bit. Why don't you join me?"

He started to shake his head again.

"Alaric. I think it would be good for you. You're no good to anyone, especially yourself, if you're wound up."

Finally, he nodded. Five minutes later they were walking down the stone path that led to the house's private dock. She stayed silent, soaking in the sounds surrounding them: the distant chirping of a bird, the soft lapping of the water against the shore as a brisk wind danced across the water, the creak of the dock as they stepped onto the wood decking.

It wasn't until they'd reached the end of the pier, gazing out over the water, that he spoke.

"I hate him."

Her heart twisted in her chest. She'd never known anything but love for her father. She couldn't imagine having a father like Daxon, let alone fathom how Alaric had turned into the man he was today with such a selfish sire.

"I hate him," Alaric repeated, his eyes distant as he stared at the mountain peaks on the other side of the lake, "yet when I heard that he was so close to death, I felt sad."

She reached out, grabbed his gloved hand. His fingers lay limp for a moment before entwining with hers.

"Understandable."

His harsh bark of laughter echoed out over the water.

"How? How is it understandable that I feel anything akin to regret for that sad excuse of a human being?" His head whipped around, his face thunderous. "He killed my mother. Not outright murder, but he brought on her heart attack. Every time he ended up in the papers, one of his mistresses on his arm, she withered away a little bit more until there was nothing left. I have no doubt that his actions caused her heart attack. The bastard didn't even visit her in the hospital, just showed up at her funeral to be in the pictures."

Clara's lips parted in shock. Daxon hadn't been as

prolific in his romantic conquests in the years she'd been with the palace. She'd heard plenty of rumors, seen old copies of newspapers. He'd leered at her the few times she'd interacted with him personally. But she'd never personally been subjugated to the torment he'd put his son and wife through.

"He couldn't have known when he created that marriage contract that Celestine would turn into the woman she became. But sometimes, when I saw the pictures of what she was doing, it was like reliving the worst years of my father's debauchery."

"Why didn't you break it off sooner?"

"I couldn't. Linnaea needed the money our marriage would bring in. It wasn't until Cass's offer of a dowry in exchange for marrying Briony that the possibility of breaking it off was on the table. Even then, I didn't want to break my word."

He said it matter-of-factly, the prince who had long ago accepted his fate to benefit his people. Her heart broke for the man who had sacrificed so much even as she felt herself falling over the edge, falling deeper for someone who had suffered time and time again to live up to his commitments.

"The more she appeared in the tabloids, the more I built my walls up. I felt nothing for her because by then I had closed myself off. But Daxon…" His voice trailed off. "There were moments growing up, times when I saw what my mother must have seen in him. It created a longing that, to this day, I still can't shake."

"He's your father." She squeezed his hand. "Even if it doesn't make sense logically, it's natural to want their love no matter how much they hurt us. There's a lot to mourn in a situation like this."

"Did you mourn Miles?"

The random question threw her. She started to pull her hand away, but he tightened his grip.

"Don't pull away from me, Clara." Sorrow made his voice heavy. "Not now."

She swallowed hard, trying to find the right words.

"In a way I did. I felt like I mourned more what I thought we had the first month we dated, the possibility of what could have been."

Alaric nodded.

"What might have been," he echoed. "Miles died outside of Chamonix in France?"

The lingering sense of nausea that was never far away spiraled upward and shot into her throat. She swallowed hard, noting his eyes flickering to her throat.

"Yes."

"A car accident."

He stumbled on his way to the car. Dropped the keys on the ground. She knew he was too drunk to drive, knew she should stop him. But she didn't. Because she was a coward.

"Yes."

He was fishing. She'd seen him use this tactic plenty of times in meetings, at political dinners, with his own father. He was good...very good at portraying himself as the one with all the answers.

She debated for a moment. If she gave him part of the truth, perhaps it would be enough to get him to back down.

"Miles was drunk." She looked down, allowing the

guilt she lived with every day to finally show. "I...we were at a party at a friend's chalet. He grabbed the keys and slapped me when I suggested I drive." She rapidly blinked away the unexpected tears burning behind her eyes. "He was angry that I suggested he not drive in front of his friends."

"We do a background check on all of our employees. Miles's death showed as part of yours. I never saw anything about him being intoxicated."

"When you have parents as wealthy as Miles, you can make the police and the media say whatever you want."

Thank God she'd had the wherewithal to get a copy of the toxicology report before they'd manipulated the truth, tried to paint her as the perpetrator of the accident.

Although it wouldn't have been far off.

Sympathy shone in Alaric's eyes, as if he finally understood her.

If only you knew the whole truth. Would you still want to make love to me? Have a child with me when I cost someone his life because I was too weak to stop him?

"You feel guilty for not stopping him."

She wanted so badly to tell him. But what if he looked at her not with the tenderness of last night but with disgust? Daxon's affairs and Celestine's partying were nothing compared to a young man losing his life.

"Yes."

The choke in her voice was real. She didn't relive those minutes as often as she used to. But certain anniversaries, like his death and their wedding, brought them back with vivid force, along with a list of *should have done this* and *could have done that*. She could have not married Miles. She should have put her foot down about him driving that night. She shouldn't have grabbed the wheel…

"I'm sorry, Clara."

"Thank you."

He scrubbed a hand over his face. "I shouldn't have sprung that on you. I needed to focus on something else. Although it helps."

"It does?"

"Yes. Being able to talk. Being with someone who understands the complex pain of losing someone you don't really like but will still mourn in a way after they're gone."

A storm of emotions descended on her. A sense of freedom at having finally shared a small part of her story. Pride that she had at last had enough confidence to speak.

But beneath that little thread of light churned something far darker and dangerous: fear. She'd opened the lock on her past and let Alaric see inside. Eventually, she would have to tell him everything. It was the right thing to do and, after what he'd shared about the impact his father's scandalous behavior had had not just on the country but on Alaric and his mother, he deserved to know what had happened, to prepare in the event that the truth of Miles's accident ever came out.

She would have to…but not just yet. Alaric had revealed the effects Daxon's and Celestine's behavior had had on his views toward love and romance. He would never be able to let himself care for her the way she was coming to care about him.

But he did feel something, some sort of affection and respect that had strengthened over the course of their honeymoon. If she revealed the full truth too soon and, worse, that she had concealed so much from him, would he ever be able to forgive her? Would their fledgling relationship survive, or would it be crushed under the weight of her deceit before it had a chance to grow?

A breeze stirred the bare branches of the trees overhead. A shiver racked her body, although whether it was the cold or her internal struggle, she couldn't say. Alaric moved behind her and wrapped his arms around her, pulling her back against his chest. She banished her frightened thoughts and sank into his embrace, focusing on the weight of his arms, the dull thud of his heartbeat against her back, the lingering scent of pine she'd come to know so well.

They stood there until the tips of their noses had turned red with cold. They returned to the house as the sky dimmed. When he paused at the bottom of the stairs, she reached out her hand. He followed her up the stairs and into her room. He kissed her slowly, undressed her even slower. She returned each caress, pressing her lips to the sensitive skin of his wrist, savored the hiss of his breath at her touch.

When he laid her back on the bed and covered her naked body with his, she parted her thighs and arched into the thrust of his hips as he slid inside her. He held her in his arms as they matched each other's rhythm, deep languid movements that slowly carried them up to the peak of pleasure.

After, he tugged her into the curve of his body, his chest pressed against her back. She listened as his breathing deepened and he slipped into sleep.

But every time she closed her eyes, sleep eluded her, chased away by the memories of that awful night when she'd yanked the wheel out of her husband's hands and sent the car careering off the road.

Would she ever escape her past?

CHAPTER FOURTEEN

BRIONY'S MOUTH DROPPED open as she walked into the lake house.

"This looks like something from the coast of Maine!"

Clara smiled. "I've never been to the States before."

"You'd love it," Briony assured her. "Little coastal towns with houses just like this. Big windows, wood interiors, porches galore." She enveloped her big brother in an enthusiastic hug. Clara watched as he returned her embrace, a smile teasing his lips.

As much as Clara had been enjoying her time with Alaric, it was good to see Briony and Cass. Briony had called asking if she and Cass could drop by on their way back to Linnaea from their own honeymoon. She'd missed her big brother, Alaric had said, the roll of his eyes belying the affection in his voice.

Clara had been apprehensive when Cass brought Alaric's long-lost half sister to the palace three months ago. Her concerns had lain primarily with Cass and what she saw as his manipulative attempts to get his family back into Linnaea. She'd been right, except that Cass had done something unexpected. He'd fallen in love with Briony.

Briony had been even more unexpected. A bartender who had paused her education degree to care for her stepfamily after her mother's unexpected death, she'd taken to royal life like she'd been born into it. She'd pursued the rebuilding of Linnaea's education system with a passion that had impressed even her stalwart brother. In just a few short months, she had proven to be what Alaric desperately needed: family.

Something he needed now more than ever Clara thought as Briony bounced over to her for a hug. Alaric had considered cutting their honeymoon short after Daxon's health scare. But the doctors had assured him that Daxon was stabilized. Having Briony's visit to look forward to and knowing she would be going back to Linnaea had helped him relax once more.

They started off most mornings with breakfast in the kitchen. Unlike the first morning when she'd come down to the professional spread laid out by the cook, Alaric cooked most mornings while she sat on a high-top chair at the counter and read. Mornings were spent tackling palace business. Even though Alaric had hired a new official executive assistant, she was performing many of the duties she had before.

Except this time, she thought with a smile, those duties were occasionally paused as she pulled the skirt of her dress up and straddled his lap, or Alaric lured her into the shower for a sensual rinse as he wrapped her legs around his waist and took her against the tiled wall. That afternoon on the dock seemed to have ripped away the last of their reticence, at least when it came to sex. They couldn't get enough of each other.

Aside from their romantic encounters, afternoons had become her favorite. They'd walked through the winding corridors of Geneva's old city center, explored the shops in Carouge shopping district and sampled fondue brought in by an exclusive restaurant in the coziness of the lake house's family room. They'd even spent one blissful afternoon planning out their new apartment at the palace, right down to the nursery decorated in a woodland theme that reminded her of the forest behind the castle.

And nights…nights they made love in her bed, falling asleep in a tangle of limbs.

It was the happiest she'd ever been in her life. So why, she asked herself as her sister-in-law wrapped her in a hug, couldn't she just be satisfied with what she had? Why was she wanting more when Alaric had made it clear that he had no interest in deepening their relationship emotionally? After his confession on the pier, there had been no more intimate talks, no more unburdening of feelings. There were times she caught him glancing at her with a slight smile, felt his touch linger as they made love.

And then there were the wedding photos. Meira and the PR office had done a spectacular job with the press release, releasing "exclusive" materials to some of the most reputable publications across the world.

The formal portraits after the ceremony had been lovely. But it had been a candid shot right before their vows, when Alaric had kissed her hand as she'd thanked him for arranging the more intimate details of their day, that had made her breath catch. The way he looked down at her, his gaze appreciative and warm as she'd smiled up at him, had confirmed the truth she'd been trying to avoid.

She'd fallen in love with her husband. She'd fallen in love, and she didn't know what to do about it.

As if she'd summoned him with her chaotic thoughts, Alaric came up behind her and slid an arm around her waist. She relaxed into his embrace.

"Dinner is ready," he announced, his voice a rumble against her back.

"Great." Briony bounced on her toes. "We barely ate on the flight over."

Cass shook his head as he smiled indulgently at his wife.

"I barely ate. Briony ate everything in sight."

Briony playfully swatted his arm. "Well, I am eating for two."

It took a moment for Briony's words to register. When they did, Clara's jaw dropped.

"You're pregnant?"

Briony nodded, her face radiant. "Sorry, we had this whole plan for telling you over dinner, but I just couldn't resist." She turned to Alaric. "You're going to be an uncle!"

Alaric swept her into a tight hug.

"Congratulations."

The rest of the evening passed in a blur. Conversation shifted from what Briony and Cass had done on their honeymoon to the upcoming treaty with Switzerland. It wasn't until after dinner, when Alaric pulled Cass aside to talk business, that Briony and Clara got a moment alone.

"I'm really happy for you and Cass," Clara said as they sipped tea by the fire.

"Thank you." Briony patted her still-flat stomach. "It's a little hard to take it all in. Finding out I'm a princess, getting married, having a baby. I feel like I've lived three lifetimes these last few months." She leaned in, a conspiratorial gleam in her eye. "I couldn't help but wonder if you and I will be giving birth about the same time."

For a moment Clara just stared at her.

"What… I don't know what you're talking about."

"I saw you the day of our wedding." She motioned toward Clara's belly. "Your hand drifted down and laid across your stomach, just like I started doing as soon as I found out. And then I remembered the night of the dinner with the Swiss ambassador and his family." Her smile turned devilish. "When you and Alaric were comforting me, I didn't fully register the implication of your hair being all mussed when I came to his office. But then it all fell into place."

"You haven't told anyone, have you?"

"No, of course not! The only reason I even told Daxon that the two of you had gotten married was because he was spouting off about contacting Alaric's ex-fiancée's father and trying to get their marriage back on track." She scowled. "Alaric never should have been engaged to her in the first place."

Clara's initial panic abated, leaving her feeling a little dizzy.

"Alaric…you should know Alaric didn't cheat on Celestine. What happened between us happened after she'd broken off their engagement."

Briony laid her hand over Clara's. "My brother is one of the most honorable people I know. I never doubted his integrity for one second. But even if the sequence of events had been different, their engagement wasn't real. And judging by the photos I saw, she was certainly not faithful to him."

Clara's lips twisted into a grimace. She'd seen plenty of photos of Celestine Osborn, but that last one, especially knowing what she did know about Alaric's past, made her livid that a woman could act so selfishly and cruelly.

"She certainly seemed to like the attention," was the nicest thing she could come up with.

"The wrong attention. Now, your photos," Briony said, her voice lightening, "those were stunning."

Clara smiled as a pleased blush stole across her cheeks. "Thank you."

"I'm so glad Alaric listened to me."

"Listened to you?"

"Yeah, about moving the ceremony…" Briony's voice trailed off as her eyes widened for a moment. "I just mentioned the rose garden seemed really nice. I spent a lot of time there when I first got to the palace."

Clara's chest tightened with pain. She'd thought Alaric had come up with the idea to move the ceremony himself. It had been the first gesture that had made her question if perhaps he saw their relationship as something more than just a business arrangement.

Except it hadn't been his idea at all.

Her chest tightened painfully.

"Did you suggest anything else?"

Briony glanced at her husband and her brother.

"I don't think—"

"Briony. Please."

Her sister-in-law's face fell. "The dress. And the photographer."

Numbness set in. Their wedding had been the moment she thought things had truly started to change. But now, to find out it had all been someone else's idea, made her feel like the biggest fool. Hadn't she just been asking why she couldn't be happy with what she and Alaric had?

"Clara, I'm sorry—"

"Briony, it's not your fault," Clara interrupted as she laid a hand over her sister-in-law's. "And it's not Alaric's, either. It was a lovely ceremony, regardless of who came up with what idea. I made an assumption and it surprised me to find out differently, that's all."

Briony watched her nervously. "Are you sure? You two seem so happy. I'd feel terrible if I ruined it with my big mouth."

Clara looked across the room as Alaric conversed with Cass. As if he'd sensed her watching him, he glanced over at her and smiled. Could she really hold a grudge for something that hadn't been done out of malice or hurt? Worse, how could she be upset with him when she hadn't been entirely truthful about her own past?

She had a husband who worshipped her in bed, made her breakfast every morning and had once more begun to treat her like a partner in work. She would be a mother before the year was out, and welcoming a niece or nephew, too.

She breathed in, her resolve strengthening. The wedding ceremony may not have been Alaric's idea. But she had so much more than she'd ever thought possible. She certainly had more with Alaric than she'd ever had with Miles.

Even if her husband didn't return her love, she had his affection and his respect. It would be enough.

It had to be.

"You didn't ruin anything, Briony." She smiled at Alaric before turning back to her sister-in-law. "I'm very happy."

Briony accepted her words with a relieved sigh and another apology before turning the topic back to baby names and nursery themes. She seemed to accept Clara's words.

If only Clara could accept them herself.

Alaric closed the door to Clara's room and turned, his body already anticipating finding his wife in bed waiting for him.

The bed was empty.

He glanced around the room, his pulse kicking up a notch. Clara had been fine until after dinner. After he'd finished talking with Cass and they'd rejoined their wives, she'd seemed a dimmer version of herself. Aloof, withdrawn, more like the Clara he had worked with for the first few years.

She'd engaged in conversation with Briony, chatted with Cass about the treaty, leaned into his touch as he'd sat next to her on the couch.

But something was different. As soon as Briony and Cass had bid them good-night, insisting on staying at a hotel in Geneva so as not to interrupt the honeymooners, she'd disappeared upstairs.

The muted sound of rushing water met his ears. He moved toward the bathroom door, pulling off his clothes as he went. It wasn't just desire guiding his steps. It was the unsettling notion that had flared up every now and then when he would catch Clara looking at him with sadness in her gaze, or staring at something in the distance, a haunted look in her eyes.

He needed to ask her. Part of him didn't want to press her or risk upsetting her. Yet he wanted to hear her answer, be reassured that she wasn't concealing something from him. The possibility that after all he'd shared with her, she hadn't trusted him with something created a gaping void in his chest that ached just at the thought of her not being honest with him.

Perhaps this was the result of giving in to his emotions more and allowing himself to experience his growing feeling of affection for his wife. It was hard not to wonder when this period of happiness would come crashing down and the next scandal or hardship would burst through the haven they'd created on the wintery shores of Lake Geneva.

He dismissed his worries as he opened the door. He moved to the shower, savoring the sight of his wife's nude body through the wavy glass. Her head was tilted back, wet hair plastered to her back as she stood beneath the waterfall stream, skin glistening. Suds clung to her full breasts as her hand drifted down, a bar of soap in her fingers.

Dear God, he was jealous of a bar of soap.

The door to the shower creaked as he stepped inside. Her eyes shot open, her lips parting in surprise before they tilted up into a small smile.

"Hi."

He stepped beneath the water and kissed her as if they'd been apart for hours instead of just minutes. She wrapped her arms around his neck, pressed her wet body against his in an intimate manner that made his hard length throb with need.

"Clara," he murmured against her lips. "Are you all right?"

She pulled back, her hands resting on his chest.

"I'm tired, but yes. It was nice seeing your sister and Prince Cass... Cass."

He chuckled at the slight wrinkling of her nose.

"It'll take some getting used to." His hand drifted up to smooth a wet tendril of hair back from her face. "You seemed down after dinner."

She blinked twice before her gaze darted off to the side, then back. A gesture so fast he would have missed it if he hadn't been watching her.

His chest tightened. There was something.

"Clara, what is it? Is the baby okay? Are you all—"

She went up on her toes and pressed her mouth to his. Her hands slid up his chest to his neck, then farther into his hair, fingers tangling in the wet strands. His arms cradled her close, his body demanding that he enjoy every bit of what she was offering even as his mind fought him, demanding answers.

"I'm fine," she whispered against his mouth between frantic kisses. "The baby is fine." She leaned back for one fleeting moment, the sadness in her eyes so acute it stabbed him to his core. "Have you ever been so happy you think there's no way it could possibly last?"

He stared at her. Had he voiced his own fears out loud? Or were they just so in tune, so much alike, that they were both terrified of accepting the happiness they'd found in this home by the water?

"Clara." His fingers firmed on her back, pulling her against his body until not even a sliver of daylight could come between them. "We've both been hurt. A lot. But that doesn't mean we're going to lose what we've created here. We're better people than the ones who hurt us, and we're not going to hurt each other the way they did."

This time her smile was more genuine, a small glimmer of her previous happiness creeping back in.

"You're right."

"I'm the prince. Of course I'm right."

He caught her laugh in another kiss, her mirth quickly turning to desire as he caressed her breasts, his hands sliding down her slick skin to part her thighs as he knelt before her and worshipped her core with his lips and tongue. She tasted so sweet, her soft cries growing louder, hips pumping against his mouth as he caressed her folds with long, slow licks.

When she came apart in his arms, he stood, hooking his arms behind her knees and lifting her up, pinning her against the tiled wall as he slid inside her. She gasped, clinging to him as he held himself deep within her.

"Alaric!"

She wrapped her legs around him and he let go of

his control, their bodies joining as water streamed over them, the shower drowning out their cries of pleasure as they came apart in each other's arms.

CHAPTER FIFTEEN

ALARIC WOKE TO what had quickly become one of the most enjoyable parts of his day: the feeling of soft, warm skin pressed against his body. A quiet murmur brought a smile to his lips as Clara shifted, one arm draped across his chest, a leg firmly secured over his thigh. Silky strands of hair grazed his neck and sent a rush of heat to his groin.

He glanced down at his sleeping wife. They'd made love three times last night, including once in the middle of the night when they'd awoken pressed together in a frenzied passion of kissing that had ended with her astride his hips, hands pressed against his chest as she'd ridden him to the most pleasurable climax he'd ever experienced. As her own pleasure had taken hold and made her cry out, he'd reached up and placed one hand on her stomach. The intimacy of their lovemaking, the knowledge that she was carrying his child inside her, had intensified the pleasure coursing through his body. He'd come with a shout, pulling her down so that her naked body was pressed against his as he claimed her lips in a possessive kiss.

He had never experienced such sexual intimacy before. Any intimacy, really. After they'd spoken on the pier, it was as if a weight had been lifted from his heart he hadn't even known he'd been carrying all these years. Spending time with Clara, touching her, listening to her voice, all of it thrilled him. With no expiration date on their relationship, with her unconditional acceptance of all of his fears, she'd set him free.

Now if he could only do the same for her. The sadness in her eyes, the fear that something would come along to wreck the happiness they'd found, made him grateful her horrific excuse for a husband was in his grave. A sentiment most would probably find cruel, but he didn't care. The man had laid his hands on Clara, had used and abused her in her time of grief. That she had not only survived but become the woman she was today was a testament to her strength and resilience.

Now if she could only do what he himself was slowly learning how to do: let go of the past and embrace the gifts of the present.

She stirred once more before rolling over, taking a good portion of the thick blanket with her. Cool air prickled his skin. He leaned over, planted a soft kiss on her bare shoulder and rolled out of bed. Much as he wanted to wake her by sliding into her wet heat and seeing her eyes flutter open with desire as he moved inside her, she needed to rest.

He tugged on his robe and, with one last look at his future queen, closed the door behind him.

Perhaps, he thought as he walked into his suite, he could suggest she move into his bedroom. They'd slept together every night since they'd first made love as husband and wife. Another intimacy he had pictured himself engaging in, but one he had quickly become addicted to.

A fact that should bother him. He had been firm in his commitment to keep emotions out of their arrangement and reserve affection for their child. But the more happiness he found in the littlest of things, from her grateful smile when he made her a slice of toast to the satisfaction of once more working together, the more he found himself embracing the feelings developing. Affection, tenderness, warmth.

Briony and Cass had fallen in love, despite all odds. Yes, his mother had been destroyed by her love for his father. But Daxon was a different beast altogether. Clara was nothing like him. She was generous and honest and cared about the people of Linnaea.

And as she'd reminded him the few times he'd revisited and voiced his deepest fear, he wasn't Daxon. He wouldn't hurt Clara the way his father had hurt his mother.

In an odd way, Daxon's prognosis had also been a balm to years of hurt and resentment. Admitting to Clara that part of him still yearned for a relationship with a man who had been so cruel and selfish, and having her offer him nothing but support and acceptance in return, had made him feel…normal. There would always be regret that he and Daxon would most likely never repair their relationship.

At least Daxon had given him one thing: the motivation to never repeat his father's mistakes.

Linnaea's future was brighter than it had ever been. His sister was happily married and expecting her own child. He was married, and to someone he enjoyed being with instead of being trapped in a loveless business arrangement. He was going to be a father. Perhaps it was time to let go of the past and move forward.

His phone rang. He glanced down, then frowned. The screen identified the call as being from the Los Angeles area. Only a select few had his direct line.

"Yes?"

"Is this Prince Alaric Van Ambrose?"

The cultured yet snooty feminine voice immediately set him on edge. Disdain dripped through the phone.

"Who's calling?"

"My name is Temperance Clemont. My son was married to your wife."

She practically spat out the word *wife*. His entire body tensed. What little Clara had shared about her former husband and her in-laws had left him with the impression that Temperance and Stanley Clemont had spoiled the hell out of their one and only child, rendering him a useless human being who had tried to exert a childish control over the woman he should have revered. Every time he remembered Clara's face, the sadness and shame when she'd revealed Miles's behavior in the minutes leading up to his fatal accident, he wanted to strangle the man for daring to lay a hand on her.

"What can I do for you, Mrs. Clemont?"

"It's not what you can do for me, Your Highness, but what I can do for you."

He rolled his eyes. "I don't have time for melodrama, Mrs. Clemont. I understand your history with my wife is not a pleasant one, but I have no interest in dredging up the past."

"Even if a scandal could rock everything you've built for your country?"

Anger started to burn deep in his chest.

"I don't take kindly to threats."

"I'm not threatening," Temperance replied coolly. "I'm merely sharing valuable information."

"That your son died because he was drinking and made the poor decision to drive?"

Silence followed his bald statement. He didn't feel the least bit guilty. The woman had somehow manipulated Clara into thinking it was her fault that Miles had died when she had raised him to never take responsibility for his own actions.

"My son died because of Clara."

The ice in Temperance's voice could have frozen hell.

"Clara had nothing to do with it. If you're saying she's responsible because she didn't stop him from driving—"

"Clara's responsible because she was in the car with Miles when it crashed. The police found her fingerprints on the wheel."

Clara woke in a pleasant daze. She reached out, her hand brushing the empty space beside her. Disappointment filled her when she opened her eyes and realized she was alone. Who would have guessed how quickly she would get used to sleeping next to and waking up with her husband after sleeping alone for her whole life?

She stretched her arms above her head, wincing as her muscles burned. She hadn't meant to share her feelings with Alaric last night. But when he'd looked at her with such tenderness, when he'd been frightened for her and the baby, she hadn't been able to stop the words from flowing.

She slowly got out of bed and headed toward the sunken hot tub. As the tub filled with warm water and relaxed the parts of her body that ached from their night of amorous lovemaking, she finally acknowledged the truth she'd been trying to deny: she needed to tell Alaric everything. All she was doing was delaying the inevitable. He deserved the truth, had deserved it before they'd said their vows. She in turn needed to trust what he had said last night before he'd claimed her body with his own, that they wouldn't lose what they had created.

It wasn't until she was getting dressed that she saw the light blinking on her phone. A quick check showed that the text was from Alaric. Her grin dimmed a bit as she read the brief message.

Please come to my office when you're awake.

She checked her reflection in the mirror, smoothed her hair and headed down the hall. Not the sweetest of messages after the night they'd had. But he was still working very hard on the deal with Switzerland. Who knew what catastrophe he could have potentially woken up to.

She knocked on the door to his office.

"Come in."

Unease whispered across the back of her neck as she opened the door and saw him standing by the window with his back to her, his hands tucked into his pockets. Just two weeks ago Alaric had opened the door for her at the palace. "Things have changed," he'd said.

Had something else happened?

Stop being negative.

"Good morning," she said warmly.

He didn't reply for what felt like the longest time. Unease grew into alarm as she noted the tension in the column of his neck, the fierce set of his shoulders.

"Alaric, what's wrong?"

"When were you going to tell me you were in the car with Miles when it crashed?"

The world dropped out from under her. Bright points of light flickered across her vision as she sucked in a deep, shuddering breath. Somewhere in the recess of her mind she heard Miles's cruel laughter as she cried out a warning, as she reached for the wheel...

"What...what do you—"

"Don't deny it."

He continued to stare out the window. His voice, low and laced with icy fury, burrowed its way under her skin and lodged in her heart.

"I'm not denying it," she finally choked out. "Alaric, please, I have to tell you—"

"How many times did I ask if there was something you needed to tell me? When I bared my soul to you, did you take everything I had to give while not trusting me with your own past? Did you share the tiniest pieces so I wouldn't ask any more questions?"

Her throat tightened as she slowly sank into a chair.

"It had nothing to do with not trusting you."

"Didn't it?"

He finally turned. She wished he hadn't. His face, the face she'd caressed last night as he'd made love to her, was frozen into a mask of fury the likes of which she'd never seen. The jaw she'd kissed was now tight, his green eyes sharp and dark. Anger radiated off him and filled the room.

"No. I was… I've never told anyone what happened."

"Not even your husband?"

Her hand came up. He eyed it as if she'd covered her skin in her poison. Her arm dropped back to her side.

"Alaric, I didn't know how to talk about it. When we were married, it was made clear that this was going to be a formal arrangement. Sharing something like that… there's so much emotion and vulnerability."

"And when I told you about my past, about what my father did to my mother, you didn't think that was me displaying some emotion and vulnerability?"

Her eyes filled with tears. "It was, and it meant so much to me."

"So much that you continued to keep a secret from me? And not just one secret."

Confusion swept through her.

"What are you talking about?"

He stalked toward her, his eyes unblinking, his movements subtle but swift. Gone was the affectionate, loving husband she'd been accustomed to, replaced by a king-to-be who had retreated behind a wall of ice. His shoulders were rigid, the tendons in his neck taut as a vein pulsed beneath his skin.

"I'm talking about your fingerprints being found on the wheel of the car."

A dull roar built in her ears. How could he have possibly found that out? Alaric's lips moved, but she didn't hear a word that came out as blood roared in her ears. The world slowed down as her mind tried to reconcile between the past and the present. A memory flashed through her mind, a vivid image of her fingers curling around the wheel as she yanked, hearing Miles's shout as he cursed her, the car veering off to the side and the tree looming up out of the rain.

"What?" she finally gasped.

"Did you know there are suspicions that you caused the car accident to rid yourself of an inconvenient husband and inherit his money?"

Betrayal robbed her of her voice as she stared at him. He returned her stare with a frigid, unblinking stare of his own.

Finally, she swallowed past the tightness in her throat.

"Do you really believe that? That I'm capable of such a crime?"

"No." Her momentary relief disappeared as he continued, "But given that I only have one side of the story to go on, that my *wife* didn't confide in me, I can only go off what I was told."

The pieces fell into place with a resounding thud that wiped away the guilt she'd been feeling over not confiding in Alaric. There was only one person in the world who would have made such a horrific accusation.

"Did you call Temperance or did she call you?"

"It doesn't matter."

She looked up at him. Whether it was the shock or some leftover semblance of self-control, she managed to keep her voice level. "It does matter. It matters who called who, and it matters that instead of giving me a chance to tell my side of what happened, you automatically went off the word of a woman you've never met, a woman I told you made my life a living hell when I was with her son."

"You had your chance. Multiple ones, in fact." His eyes flickered. "I told you how important it's been to rise above the gossip Daxon and Celestine courted for years. I told you what the tabloids and press did to my mother. You know personally how much is riding on Linnaea being shown as a country rising from the ashes, not a nation run by spoiled despots. What do you think the media will do if they find out I not only married my secretary after I got her pregnant the night my fiancée broke off our engagement, but that I married a woman suspected of causing the accident that killed her wealthy husband?"

I won't cry. I will not cry.

Slowly, she stood.

"Is that what's most important here? Preserving Linnaea's image?"

"Don't twist my words," Alaric growled. "That's a part of it. You lied to me."

"I never lied."

"Concealed, distorted, however you did it, you didn't tell me the truth, Clara."

She closed her eyes to keep the tears at bay. She should have told him, should have trusted that he would listen to her as she had listened to him when he'd confided so much in her. But she'd done exactly what he'd told Cass not to: let her fears hold her back.

Now it was too late. She'd broken Alaric's trust. Temperance would never let her stop paying for what she imagined Clara had done to her precious son. The happiness Clara had so briefly found with her husband would now be forever out of reach. She could try to explain, but he'd just revealed he cared more about reputation and scandal than he did the truth.

She breathed in deeply and opened her eyes.

"Since Temperance filled you in on the details, it sounds like there's nothing more for me to say."

She turned and started for the door.

"Do not walk away from me, Clara. We aren't finished here."

"But we are." She stopped, her hand on the doorknob, and looked back at him. "You already have all the information you need. If it comes to light in the press, I'll work with the public relations department to mitigate the fallout as much as possible and will take full responsibility for whatever is needed to preserve Linnaea's image."

He ran a hand through his hair, the first sign that he wasn't in full control of his emotions.

"It's not just a public relations issue."

"No, but that seems to be a priority. Why else would you have taken Briony's suggestion to move the ceremony or take the wedding photos?"

She waited for him to correct her, to tell her it had been more than just for publicity.

But he remained silent, watching her with that hawklike gaze.

Her hurt surged forth, took control of her tongue.

"Caring about how things look compared to how they are seems to run in the family."

She wanted to snatch the words back as soon as they left her mouth. His lips parted slightly as the full weight of what she'd said registered, essentially accusing him of his worst fear: that he was just like his father.

But before she could even begin to apologize, he pointed at the door.

"Go. The helicopter will be here in an hour to take you back to Linnaea." He bit out the words with a snapping fury that made her tremble. "We'll revisit this issue in time. But until I summon you, I don't want to hear from you, see you, nothing."

"Alaric, I—"

"You will refer to me as 'Your Highness.'" He walked around his desk and sat, focusing his gaze on his computer. "First names are for couples who share something beyond a formal arrangement."

"But I..."

Her voice trailed as the words welled in her throat.

I love you. I'm so sorry. I should have trusted you, trusted myself. I love you so much, Alaric.

"I'm sorry, Alaric," she finally whispered.

He didn't even look up.

"Goodbye, Your Highness."

CHAPTER SIXTEEN

THE MOUNTAINS OF Linnaea glittered in the distance. Clara kept her gaze focused on the snowcaps as the train rolled into the station. When the helicopter had arrived at the airport in Geneva, she'd taken one look at the private plane they'd flown in on and nearly burst into tears. Between the rapid unraveling of her relationship with Alaric and the pregnancy hormones, the thought of flying in the plane she'd flown with her husband on as they'd begun their honeymoon had been too much.

Stefan, poor man, had said he had to get permission from Alaric and the head of security. Clara had calmly told him she would scream that she was being kidnapped unless he took her to the station. Fortunately, he had obliged. She'd texted Meira a note to send him a bonus with his next check. He was good at his job, and he didn't deserve getting caught between two feuding monarchs.

A chill swept under the door of her private car as passengers walked past to disembark. Her skin pebbled beneath the thick wool of her sweater, but she barely noticed. She felt as cold inside as the ice glittering on the branches outside her window.

Had it been just twenty-four hours ago that she'd been cocooned in the warmth of her husband's arms after he'd made love to her? How had everything they'd been building over the past month fallen apart so quickly?

Simple. There wasn't anything between the two of you except a baby and good sex.

A lump rose in her throat. She knew better. Alaric may have felt nothing. But despite the cruel words she'd flung at him like daggers as she'd left, she loved him. She loved him so much it hurt.

Her phone buzzed in her pocket. She pulled it out to see an unfamiliar number on the screen. The text beneath alerted her to the fact that the call was from Los Angeles. Her chest constricted. Only two people would be contacting her from Los Angeles, and she had zero desire to speak with either of them. If Temperance Clemont was standing in front of her right now, it would be very hard not to slap what would no doubt be a very smug, self-satisfied expression off her face.

She sent the call to voice mail. A moment later, when it rang again, she turned her phone off.

Temperance may have succeeded in destroying what little relationship had been developing between Clara and her husband. But she would not let that vile woman have any more power over her life.

A private car whisked her from the train station to the palace. When she reached the floor that housed the royal family's apartments, she stopped. Where did she belong? The family suite she and Alaric had begun to decorate together from afar? Alaric's private apartment?

It could have been seconds or an hour before she

slowly turned and took the elevator back down to her old apartment. The door swung open and, thankfully, her things were still in place. It would cause more gossip when she notified the palace staff that she would be remaining in her old suite until further notice. But given the media storm that was about to descend on the palace, she found she didn't really care anymore what others thought. Alaric had sworn he wouldn't divorce her. The next few months would be ugly, but eventually another royal would do something foolish or get married or have a baby. The spotlight would move off her and Linnaea. Alaric would continue to make progress in rebuilding Linnaea. And she would do whatever was needed to ensure she never hurt him or the people of her adopted country again.

Telling herself that didn't ease her heartache. Slowly, she eased herself into her favorite chair, the chair she'd been sitting in when Alaric had approached her with the pregnancy test in hand. That night, she'd thought there was no possible way she could ever co-parent with Alaric, let alone marry him.

Now she was over a thousand miles away from her husband missing him and the promise of a beautiful life together. She'd hurt him, not once but twice. He thought she'd lied to him. Even though she hadn't outright lied, she'd certainly concealed the truth. She'd known how much he abhorred scandal. He'd given her numerous opportunities to share what had happened, had shared his worst pains and biggest vulnerabilities with her.

And in a moment of pain, she'd hurled the cruelest thing she could have possibly said. If there had been any possible hope for reconciliation in the future, she'd ruined it with her nasty parting words.

...it was easier for him to stay withdrawn because getting involved was too scary...

She had wanted the benefits of a marriage without making the same investment Alaric had, withholding the worst parts of her own past out of fear while taking everything he had offered. She'd let her own guilt over not stopping Miles from driving, from spurring her to take action too late to save his life, prevent her from telling the man she loved the truth.

Alaric had been right. She hadn't trusted him to be fair, to listen to her. She'd let fear rule her. Rule her and ruin her.

She brushed a stray tear from her cheek. Even though it hurt, the truth was finally out. She wouldn't have to move forward with the specter of his abuse and the circumstances of how he'd died looming in the background, overshadowing her new life.

That was a task she would start tomorrow. Tonight, she would mourn.

Silence greeted Alaric as he walked into the royal apartment. A quick glance confirmed what his new executive assistant, Geoffrey, had told him: Clara hadn't moved in. At first, when Geoffrey had called to report that Clara had ordered dinner be served to her in her old suite, he'd almost called her.

But what would have been the point? He'd told her that until he summoned her, he wanted nothing to do with her. She was following his orders.

It had been two days since Clara fled Lake Geneva.

Two of the longest days of his life. The lake house had changed from a haven to a haunting reminder of the happy memories he'd created with his wife over the past few weeks. Memories that, even after he'd decided to return to Linnaea, had followed him on the plane ride home.

In the hours after he'd banished Clara, he'd been righteous in his anger, whipping through one task after another with ruthless efficiency. He had told her not once but twice how much his father's scandalizing had hurt him, had shared the most vulnerable parts of his past as he'd opened up to someone for the first time. And how had she repaid him? By keeping a scandalous secret from him. She had to have known something like that wouldn't stay hidden forever, especially now that she'd been thrust into the international spotlight.

He'd stayed up until nearly two in the morning when his eyelids had drooped and he hadn't been able to keep his head up. Somehow he'd slept until the sun crested over the horizon. The next thirty-six hours had passed in a blur of virtual meetings, phone calls and emails. He ate at his desk, typed brisk orders to Geoffrey and ordered the skeleton staff to leave him alone.

It worked until he'd woken up this morning, gotten out of bed and found one of Clara's silk robes tangled in the sheets.

How weak did it make him that he missed her? That he craved seeing her smile, holding her in his arms, talking with her about revisions the Swiss ambassador had made to the proposed treaty? His mother had longed for the Daxon she'd known briefly during their courtship, the man she thought she had fallen in love with.

How many times had she said, "I just remember how things were. I know they can be better again."

Slowly, he walked down the hall to the suite of bedrooms. Three in total: a master suite with a bay of windows that overlooked the lake behind the palace and the mountains in the distance. A slightly smaller bedroom with equally stunning views.

But it was the third bedroom that made his chest tighten with pain. This bedroom had a connecting door to the master suite. This was the room for which Clara had picked out the soft green paint to serve as a backdrop for the white tree decals that re-created the forest behind the palace.

His fists clenched as he looked around the room. Clara had shared pictures she'd accumulated, from the white crib to the matching rocker in the corner next to a bookshelf stuffed with used children's books. He'd never thought about a nursery before. Nurseries were where babies slept, had their nappies changed and were nursed by their mothers.

But as Clara had talked about everything she'd envisioned taking placing in that room, the stories that would be read, the laughter that would echo off the walls, he'd found himself getting excited about a baby's room. Not just the room, but the sparkle in Clara's eyes as she'd talked, the affectionate way her hand had settled on her stomach as she'd talked about their child.

Had he been so blind as to her true nature? Or had Clara just made a terrible mistake, one that he'd overreacted to?

He surveyed the room one last time before turning and closing the door with more force than he'd intended.

When Temperance had told him about Clara being in the car, his first reaction had been hurt. He had asked Clara multiple times if there was anything in her past that he should be aware of. He hadn't said anything about not marrying her, not providing for their child. He just wanted to know. He thought, too, that she had trusted him when she had shared Miles's drunken state before he'd gotten behind the wheel. It had been why he'd felt safe opening up to her after finding out about Daxon's prognosis.

Finding out that she had kept the full circumstances from him, not given him the chance to hear her side when he had bared the darkest parts of his soul to her, had been a stab in the back.

A shrill ring cut through the stillness. He pulled his phone out of his pocket and glanced at the screen. Ronan had taken it personally that he had missed the true circumstances of Clara's husband's death and had promised Alaric an update before midnight.

Alaric closed his eyes for a moment. Did he want to know what had truly happened?

He answered.

"Yes?"

"I've got it, sir."

"Good. When can I see it?"

"One of my men is being admitted to the palace as we speak. He has a hard copy of the file. I didn't want to send it via email."

His hand tightened on the phone.

"Is it that bad?"

Ronan paused.

"Yes, Your Highness. It's bad."

Fifteen minutes later, Alaric was sitting in his office with a black file in hand, Ronan Security's initials tamped in red in the corner. He kept his gaze averted from the desk. He should have had it replaced before he left Lake Geneva.

He stared down at the folder. What would he find inside? As angry as he'd been the day he and Clara had fought, he hadn't for one second believed her capable of the accusation Temperance had leveled at her.

Didn't show it very well, did you?

The voice of his conscience whispered in his ear as he remembered Clara's beautiful blue eyes dull and wide with shock. He'd known as he'd berated her that he was being too harsh, that it wasn't so much the potential scandal that had dug its ugly talons into his heart but pain. He had started to open his heart to his wife. Finding out her deepest secret not from her but from her ex-mother-in-law had felt like a betrayal.

Slowly, he opened the folder. His heart stopped. The first image inside was of the car, a mangled black mess wrapped around a tree. In the background was Clara, strapped to a gurney as she was being loaded into an ambulance. Her face was covered in blood and scratches, her eyes barely open, tears streaking down her cheeks.

He ran a finger over her face as nausea built in his gut. His wife had gone through hell, first with a spoiled, abusive husband and then this. And how had he responded? By focusing on himself, on his pain and his past.

He spent an hour reviewing the contents of the folder. The initial report stated that Miles had had a blood alcohol content three times the legal limit. An interview conducted with Clara in the hospital revealed that Miles had been driving recklessly, weaving back and forth across the road. Clara had begged him to stop. He'd steered toward another car. She'd grabbed the wheel, yanked it to prevent the other car from being hit. Unfortunately, she'd yanked too hard. Miles had lost control of the car and wrapped it around a tree. Other drivers on the road had corroborated Clara's account, stating that the car had been moving erratically for several kilometers.

Ronan had included a letter at the back. Within twenty-four hours, the Clemonts had bought the original report and paid off multiple officers and witnesses. One officer had kept a copy of the original and quit the department over the higher-ups allowing the Clemonts to change the narrative. When Ronan had started to dig deeper, he'd come across the officer's employment records and found that he'd quit shortly after the accident. Ronan had found him relatively easily living in Spain. The officer had been more than happy to provide the original report to Ronan and let the truth come out. He'd described Temperance and Stanley Clemont as "ruthless" and "heartless" when it came to their daughter-in-law.

They cared more about their son's reputation than they ever cared about her. She nearly died trying to save lives. But they tried to paint her as a murderess.

His body grew heavy with each passage he read until he could barely move. How could he have ever doubted her? How could he have been so cruel to her?

By the time he was done, he wanted nothing more

than to run up to Clara's apartment, break down the door and beg her forgiveness.

He forced himself to stand and move to the window. Her parting insult had been accurate. Instead of acting rationally, he'd given in to his own pain and his own fear that once again scandal would plague his rule. He hadn't stopped to think about how differently Clara's circumstances had been: a woman caught up in a desperate situation created by her abusive spouse instead of his father's and ex-fiancée's self-indulgences.

Bile rose in his throat. Did he deserve her? One of his greatest fears had been that he was secretly like his father, that he would eventually cause Clara the kind of pain Daxon had caused Marianne. Hadn't he done just that with his actions over the last few days?

You are not your father.

How many times had she said that to him? He'd started to believe it before Temperance's phone call. Was he going to let people like Temperance, Celestine and Daxon ruin a future with the woman he loved?

Because he did love her, he realized with sudden clarity. He'd been falling in love with her for months. The intimacy they'd developed during their honeymoon had pushed him closer to acknowledging the depth of his feelings. Feelings he'd run from like a coward at the first sign of trouble.

As angry as he'd been at Celestine the night their engagement had ended, he really should be thanking her. If it hadn't been for the tumultuous conclusion to their arrangement, he never would have kissed Clara, never would have allowed himself to explore the emotions he felt for her.

Never would have finally opened his heart to love.

He flipped through the folder back to the first picture. Clara had been through so much: losing both her parents at a young age, going through an abusive marriage, restarting her life after a traumatic tragedy. And now he'd put her through another trauma. Did he deserve her?

No. No, he didn't. But he would spend the rest of his life trying to earn back her trust and, God willing, her love.

CHAPTER SEVENTEEN

CLARA WALKED THROUGH the rose garden, her boots crunching softly in the snow. Every time she'd woken up, which had seemed to be every hour, she'd grabbed her phone and checked the media sites to see if anything had been posted.

Nothing.

Around dawn she'd given up on sleep and gotten dressed in fleece-lined pants, a cozy sweater and her blue peacoat. Thin gray clouds covered the sky, creating a muted glow as the sun rose behind them. The palace had been quiet as she'd taken the elevator down to the ground floor and slipped out into the rose garden.

She ran a gloved hand over the leaves of the hedge. Just last month, she'd said her vows in this garden. If she'd known what was going to happen, would she have gone through with it?

Yes.

It was an easy answer. Those blissful weeks with Alaric, falling deeper in love and being loved in return for the first time in her life, were too precious to give up.

Alaric had come home last night. She'd been in her small window seat that overlooked the long drive that came up to the palace. When he'd alighted from the car, she'd pressed her face against the cold glass, drinking in the sight of him. She wanted to run to him, to throw her arms around his neck and be swept up into his embrace as she apologized for not trusting him. Perhaps, if he would have looked up, she would have done just that.

But he hadn't. He'd leaned in, said something to a dark-haired man she assumed was his new assistant—Geoffrey something—and strode into the palace. As if nothing in his life had changed.

She'd stayed in the window seat for another hour, staring out at the darkening sky, until hunger had sent her to the kitchen to scrounge for crackers and broth. Whether it was the events of the past few days, the pregnancy or both, she'd barely been able to keep any food down. It didn't help that at least once a day, Temperance tried to call her. The first couple of times, she hadn't left a voice mail. When she finally had, the accented voice had been smug.

"I warned you that you would one day pay for what happened to Miles."

The second and third voice mails had been a touch more emotional, as if Clara was offending Temperance by not responding and letting her vent her rage. She contemplated changing her number. But someone with Temperance's wealth, who probably had more money than the entire country of Linnaea, would just get her new number.

Better to let her tire herself out. She hadn't released anything to the media yet. Maybe she never would. To share that Clara was in the car that night would mean risking the discovery of Miles's state when he had been behind the wheel.

Her heart clenched. If only Alaric had talked to her instead of jumping to the worst conclusion. She could understand his hurt, see how he could have perceived her silence as a form of lying. But she couldn't understand why he'd immediately jumped to the worst possible conclusion. Even if he didn't love her, did he truly think so little of her after all this time?

Stop thinking about it. The more she ruminated, the more upset she would get. She didn't need that for herself or her child.

She sat down on one of the stone benches and looked around the garden. Right now, the pain was intense, especially when her eyes flickered to the spot where she'd exchanged vows with Alaric and he'd surprised her with that gentle kiss on the lips. But the pain would fade with time. She would instead focus on the good that had come out of their union. A slight smile tugged at her lips. Spring mornings spent on a blanket with their child, reading books and eating strawberries as the gentle scent of roses wafted around them. Or perhaps lying in the grass during summer and watching the star-filled sky.

She may not have the life she'd thought she would. But it could still be a good one.

"It's a beautiful place, even in winter."

His voice froze her in place. Had she imagined it? That deep, rich timbre of his voice as it washed over her and sent her pulse pounding?

Slowly, she turned her head. He stood just a few feet away, his hands clasped behind his back, his dark hair dusted with snow. Her throat tightened. God, she'd missed him.

"It is."

Her fingers curled around the seat of the bench. The coldness from the stone seeped through her gloves. No matter what, she would not make a fool of herself. They had to see each other eventually. Best to get it over with and move on.

"You look very pale."

She frowned.

"It is winter."

Alaric shook his head. "That's not… I meant you don't look well."

"The words every woman wants to hear when she's tired and nauseous."

Her nose wrinkled and she looked away. Great. Less than thirty seconds in each other's company and they were already snipping at each other. Was this how the rest of their marriage was destined to be?

She heard Alaric approach, shifted to the left as he eased himself onto the bench beside her to keep some space between them.

"You haven't been sleeping."

She shook her head.

She started as his hand slid over hers and gently eased her grip off the bench. She bit down on her lower lip as he threaded his fingers through hers. The simple act made her ache. Was he trying to punish her? Or was he trying to keep her calm before he dropped another bombshell on her, like asking for a divorce?

Her stomach rolled. Amazing how just three weeks ago she'd been fighting him against getting married.

Now the thought of not having him in her life in any capacity left her shaken.

"I hurt you."

Her head snapped up.

"What?"

Alaric's eyes latched onto hers, his gaze moving over her face as if he hadn't seen her in decades instead of days. Slowly, his other hand came up. When she didn't move, his fingers settled on her cheek, cradling her with a gentleness that made her eyes grow hot.

"I hurt you, Clara. I let my own pride and pain and past overrule everything else." His voice grew thick as he leaned in, resting his forehead against hers. His breath came out fast and warmed her cheek. "Can I ever begin to tell you how sorry I am?"

She sat there, frozen in place, not wanting to pull away from his touch but unsure of how to answer.

"Clara, please say something."

The sorrow in his voice yanked her out of her shock. She leaned back, missed the warmth of his skin against hers as the winter air swirled around them. She had never in a thousand years imagined that he would apologize. Hope flickered in her chest.

But hope and apologies weren't enough. If this was the beginning of a new chapter, there had to be trust and communication.

She stood, gave his hand a squeeze and walked over to the fountain. She wrapped her arms around her waist as the words spilled forth.

"Miles was drunk a lot. I knew he'd struggled when we dated, but Temperance and Stanley managed it. I wanted to have a family again so badly that I looked past so many warning signs. Even when they became big flashing neon lights telling me to get out, I hung on. I'd put so much time in, I told myself, and perhaps things would get better when we got married."

She closed her eyes, remembering the shattering of glass the night of their honeymoon when he'd hurled a champagne flute at the wall in their hotel suite because she'd asked him to stay with her instead of going back to the reception to drink more.

"I was so stupid."

She sensed rather than heard Alaric stand.

"Plenty of people have made similar mistakes, Clara."

"They have. But this was my life. I knew better." She sucked in a shuddering breath. "Have you ever noticed how, once you've made excuses for one thing, it's easier to make excuses for the bigger things that follow? It starts with one too many drinks at dinner and ends with letting your husband drive away from a party drunk."

"With you in the car."

Anger pulsed in every word. But not, she realized with relief, at her. No, Alaric was angry at Miles for putting her in that position.

"I knew he'd had too much to safely drive. I'd asked him if he was safe to drive. He pulled me aside and slapped me across the face for embarrassing him in front of his friends."

Alaric's hands cupped her shoulders. She wanted to lean back into his embrace, to draw strength from his presence. But not yet. She needed to get this out, needed him to know the full story.

"I was so shocked and humiliated that I just got in the car." Her voice caught. "I got in the car, Alaric. I put all those people on the road at risk because I was embarrassed for myself. If I had put my foot down, Miles would still be alive. I didn't realize how truly drunk he was until he started weaving back and forth across the road."

She could still see the lines on the road, blurred by the falling rain and Miles's ever-increasing speed, disappear as he drifted across the road. She'd called out his name, seen him start then laugh off her discomfort as he'd pressed down on the gas pedal. He'd told her she was boring as he'd started deliberately going back and forth, nearly clipping the bumper of the car in front of them before speeding around them and almost crashing head-on into an oncoming truck.

"He kept going faster and faster. Another car was coming and he...he said if I would just trust him, he would get close without hitting them. That it was all a game."

She'd woken up to the sound of his shrill laughter echoing in her ears for weeks after the crash.

"I wasn't trying to hurt him. I grabbed the wheel..." Her hand drifted out, mimicking her actions from that awful night so long ago. "I didn't mean to yank as hard as I did. I was just so scared..."

Alaric's arms came around her, tight and strong. She should have resisted, but she couldn't anymore. She sagged back into his embrace, letting her head drop back against his chest.

"The last thing I remember is him shouting at me right before this awful screech, metal being ripped apart as the windshield shattered in front of my eyes. When I woke up, I was in the back of an ambulance being taken to the hospital."

Silence fell as Alaric held her. Snow drifted down, tiny flakes that dusted the sleeves of his jacket. The blanket of white snuffed out all sound and cocooned them within their own quiet corner of the world.

"What did Miles's parents do?"

She swallowed back the hurt that lodged in her throat as she remembered the first time Temperance and Stanley had walked into her room.

"I thought they were coming to support me. I was so grateful to see them. But then Temperance told me it was my fault that Miles had died, that I should have done more to stop him. When I told her that I had tried, she said I hadn't tried hard enough." She turned her head, snuggled into the curve of his neck. "When the police told her I had yanked the wheel away from Miles, she accused me of murdering him for his money."

Alaric spun her around with such speed she barely caught her breath before he drew her back into his embrace, one hand coming up to cradle the back of her head as he pressed his lips against her forehead.

"I'm sorry, Clara."

His words washed over her, loosened the knot inside her chest.

"Thank you. I never meant to cause the accident. But I always wondered what if…" She sucked in a shuddering breath. "What if I had stood up to him? Wondered if Miles would still be alive. I didn't murder him, but I still killed him."

It was the first time she'd said the words out loud. They hung in the air, her full confession lingering between them.

She nearly came undone when he pressed the softest of kisses to her forehead.

"You made the only decision you could in one of the worst situations anyone could ever find themselves in. The only person responsible for Miles's death that night is Miles."

She sagged against him. He was offering her absolution, and, oh, how she wanted to accept it. But she had to make sure, one last time, that he fully understood what she'd done.

"I… I should have stopped him before he got in the car—"

"You were in a very abusive relationship, Clara. I saw my own mother withdraw into herself and make questionable decisions. Abuse strips us of who we are and leaves us with almost nothing to stand on." He kept one arm securely around her waist as he leaned back, capturing her gaze with his as he gently laid a hand on her cheek. "But you survived. You survived and look how strong you've become. I have no doubt the woman I married wouldn't hesitate now to step in if she saw someone in a position like that again."

A slow, tentative smile spread across her face even as tears finally escaped to trace their way down her cheeks.

"What changed your mind?"

"I already knew I'd made a colossal error before I got back to Linnaea. And then I reviewed the original file of the accident."

Her mouth dropped open. "But... I thought Temperance and Stanley had them all destroyed. I managed to get a copy of the toxicology report that showed Miles was drunk, but everything else... I thought it had been destroyed."

"One of the officers kept it." He placed another kiss on her forehead. "Clara... I can't imagine what you went through. I knew you were strong, but seeing what you experienced that night, and then having to deal with that witch in the aftermath..." He leaned back, a sad smile on his handsome face. "You don't know how strong you truly are, do you?"

"Just as you don't realize what an incredible leader you are."

Wind whipped around the corner of one of the hedges before he could answer. Clara shivered.

"Let's go inside. We can talk more where it's warmer."

She let him grab her hand and lead her back inside the palace. It was still early, but already she could hear the distant clang of pots in the royal family kitchen where a small staff was putting together breakfast for Alaric, Daxon and some of the higher-ranked officials who lived in the palace. A vacuum whirred down the hall as Alaric led her to elevator. A palace guard rounded the corner and stopped, standing back at attention until Alaric waved for him to be on his way. She didn't miss the slight hint of a smile on the guard's lips as his eyes drifted down to hers and Alaric's joined hands.

Linnaea had started out as a place to escape to, to put distance between her and London. But somewhere along the line it had become home.

Please let it continue to be home, she prayed as the elevator ascended. *Please let it not be too late for us to become a family.*

It took her a moment to realize that the elevator had taken them a couple floors above her apartment. As the doors whooshed open, she realized they were standing outside the door of the king's family apartment.

"Alaric…"

He turned and, before she could say another word, dropped to one knee.

"Clara, we have a lot to talk about. I have a lot to apologize for."

"So do I," she said shakily. "I should have told you—"

"Yes, you should have," he cut in gently, "but I should have trusted you." He reached out and grabbed her other hand in his. "But I'm going to do things differently moving forward. If you'll let me."

"Let you?"

"As your husband. Clara, would you do me the honor of letting me be your husband and show you every day how much I want you in my life?"

She couldn't hold back the tears this time. But at least they were happy tears, she thought as she nodded. He stood, cradled her face once more in his hands and kissed her. It was a kiss that nearly knocked her off her feet as his lips moved over hers, firm and possessive and yet so gentle and loving.

He pulled back. Before she could say another word, he opened the doors to the apartment, swept her into his arms and carried her across the threshold. The furniture was draped in plastic covers, the floor speckled with plaster dust, the walls half coated in paint.

She'd never seen anything so wonderful in her whole life.

"We'll be moved in by the end of next week," he said as he carried her up the curving stairs and down the hall. "I never want to spend another night without you in our bed."

She sighed contentedly and relaxed in his arms. "Our bed" had a lovely ring to it.

"Alaric, about what I said before I left—"

"You were right, Clara."

"But I wasn't! You are nothing like your father, Alaric."

He stopped in front of one of the doors and gently set her on her feet.

"I'm not. But in that moment, I was." He grabbed her hands and held them tightly in his grasp. "My history with my father, seeing what the negative press did to my mother, made me react in the worst way possible. I was hurt that you hadn't confided in me, angry after I'd shared what I had with you." He held up a finger as her lips parted to speak. "But that wasn't fair. Just because I chose to share something with you did not make you beholden to share with me."

"It wasn't that I didn't trust you. I just… I had never

told anyone else what happened. I was so ashamed. I hadn't forgiven myself, so how could I possibly ask you to forgive me or understand what happened?"

"There's nothing to forgive, Clara. At least nothing I need to forgive you for. All I can ask is that you forgive me." He brought one of her hands up to his lips and pressed a kiss to her fingers. "I can't promise I won't say anything hurtful the rest of our lives, or that I won't make mistakes. But I can promise I will try every day to be the kind of husband you deserve and the father our child needs."

"And I will try to be the kind of wife who will support you and your country."

His proud smile filled her with warmth.

"You are already the queen Linnaea needs."

Before she could reply, he reached over and twisted the knob. The door swung open and her breath caught. The walls were painted a soft green. A white rocking chair sat in one corner, and a bookcase next to it was filled with books. Clara walked over to it, her chest nearly bursting with happiness as she saw the signs of love in the worn spines, the slightly faded covers.

"You remembered."

"Every word. In a few months, I'll sit in here and read to our son or daughter." He gestured to the rest of the empty room. "The rest of what we picked out is on its way. It should be here in—"

She cut him off by flinging her arms around his neck and planting a passionate kiss on his lips. He groaned and pulled her flush against his body, his hardness pressing against her core. She writhed against him, savoring the tightening of his arms around her waist.

"I think it's time, my love, for us to finally be together in our marital bed."

"My love?" she repeated softly.

He smiled, a genuine smile full of happiness and warmth.

"I forgot that part, didn't I?" He leaned down and pressed a sweet kiss to the corner of her mouth. "I love you, Clara."

"You do?"

"Very, very much. I think I have for a while. It just took time for me to see it."

Clara laughed. "Wait until I tell Meira."

Alaric frowned. "Meira?"

"She told me on our wedding day that she thought there was more between us than just a working relationship. She was right. I love you, Alaric. I've loved you for so long, and I'll never stop."

He led her into what would be their first bedroom together. Everything was just as they had planned two weeks ago, down to the oversize bed draped in cozy blankets. He undressed her with infinite care, trailing kisses from her neck over her breasts, lingering on her nipples before continuing down over the soft swell of her belly. When he pressed a hot, open-mouthed kiss to her core, she nearly came undone, her fingers tangling in his hair as she moaned his name. He lifted her up as if she were made of glass, laid her on the bed and made quick work of his own clothes before he covered her naked body with his. As he slid inside her, their bodies joining in a slow, sensual dance, she reached up and pressed her hand to his cheek.

"I love you, Alaric."

"And I love you, Clara." He leaned down and sealed their pledge with a kiss.

EPILOGUE

Six months later

CLARA RELAXED ON the chaise longue, shielding her eyes against the late-morning sun as she watched her husband lay out a checkered blanket.

"You really went all out for this picnic," she teased as he reached into the wicker basket.

"If we're going to have a picnic, we're going to do it right." He leaned over and cut off any further teasing with a firm kiss. "Who knows when we'll get a chance to have alone time again?"

He gestured at her belly, round and full. In less than four weeks, their daughter would be making her appearance into the world. It had been Alaric's idea for them to have one last getaway before they officially became parents.

She leaned back against the pillows he'd arranged for her and gazed out over the sparkling waters of Lake Geneva. They'd been to the lake house every other month since they'd reconciled that wintery morning. Some trips had only been for a couple days, while others, like their glorious trip in spring, had been over a week.

It had also been a haven for two major events: Daxon's passing and the revelation of Clara's role in the car accident.

Daxon's passing had, unfortunately, been expected. He'd deteriorated quickly following Alaric and Clara's reconciliation and wound up in hospice care. As he was confined to his suite in the palace, Alaric and Briony had attempted to resolve their issues with their father. Alaric had come out tense and resigned. Briony had shook her head sadly when Clara had asked if she'd found the closure she'd been seeking.

"No. Sometimes people don't change. It's hard to accept that." She'd hugged Clara. "But we tried."

Daxon had passed two days later. Despite all the damage he'd wrought on Linnaea, Alaric and Briony had agreed to hold the customary funeral services honoring the passing of the King.

Alaric's coronation ceremony had been scheduled to take place two weeks after that. When he'd suggested they go public with the details of Clara's accident ahead of the ceremony, she'd panicked. Temperance's calls had decreased, but she had still left the occasional threatening voice mail, usually after an article had been published about her and Alaric or some picture had circulated on social media of them visiting one of Briony's schools or touring one of the many new manufacturing plants Alaric was overseeing.

There had been so much good happening for the country that the thought of her own past wreaking havoc on everything Alaric and his people had worked for her had nearly sent her into a tailspin.

"But what about the treaty? What about the fallout for Linnaea with all the media attention?"

"It's up to you, Clara. But this way, we can get everything out in the open. You have nothing to hide. Your people love you." He'd kissed her forehead. "I love you. We'll stand by you."

They'd given an exclusive interview to a star writer the week before the coronation. She hadn't shared everything. Miles had still been her husband, and she had no desire to air all of his transgressions. But she had given an abbreviated version of what had happened that night, including that in her attempts to stop Miles from driving, they'd lost control of the car.

The interview had gone viral. While there had been some negative attention, the majority of the commentary had been incredibly supportive. When Briony had told an inquisitive reporter how brave her sister-in-law was to share her own experience and how she was doing even more by overseeing the development of a medical support system for alcoholics and their loved ones, the media had gone crazy. Donations to the newly established Linnaean Alcohol Recovery Group had surpassed seven figures in less than a week.

The calls from Temperance had stopped.

A sudden kick made Clara smile. Her hand drifted down to the swell of her belly as her daughter moved inside her. Part of her would always feel sorry for Temperance. The closer she came to giving birth, the more she couldn't imagine the hell Temperance and Stanley had gone through in losing their only child.

But, she reminded herself, she and Alaric would raise

a daughter who was not only loved but knew how to treat others.

Alaric laid out plates of cheeses, strawberries and *basler brunsli*, the best chocolate cookies she'd ever eaten. He handed her a glass of sparkling grape juice.

"What are you thinking?"

She smiled. "That I'm really happy."

He clinked his glass to hers.

"You deserve every bit of happiness, my love."

* * * * *

Blown away by the drama in
The Prince's Pregnant Secretary?
Don't miss out on the first installment in
The Van Ambrose Royals duet,
A Cinderella for the Prince's Revenge

Available now!

And make sure to catch these other stories
by Emmy Grayson!

His Billion-Dollar Takeover Temptation
Proof of Their One Hot Night
A Deal for the Tycoon's Diamonds

Available now!

WE HOPE YOU ENJOYED
THIS BOOK FROM
H HARLEQUIN
PRESENTS

Escape to exotic locations where passion knows no bounds.

Welcome to the glamorous lives of royals and billionaires, where passion knows no bounds. Be swept into a world of luxury, wealth and exotic locations.

8 NEW BOOKS AVAILABLE EVERY MONTH!

HPHALO2021

COMING NEXT MONTH FROM

⊞HARLEQUIN
PRESENTS

#4057 CARRYING HER BOSS'S CHRISTMAS BABY
Billion-Dollar Christmas Confessions
by Natalie Anderson
Violet can't forget the night she shared with a gorgeous stranger. So the arrival of her new boss, Roman, almost has her dropping an armful of festive decorations. *He's* that man. Now she must drop the baby bombshell she discovered only minutes earlier!

#4058 PREGNANT PRINCESS IN MANHATTAN
by Clare Connelly
Escaping her protection detail leads Princess Charlotte to the New York penthouse of sinfully attractive Rocco. But their rebellious night leaves innocent Charlotte pregnant...and with a Christmas proposal she *can't* refuse.

#4059 THE MAID THE GREEK MARRIED
by Jackie Ashenden
Imprisoned on a compound for years, housemaid Rose has no recollection of anything before. So when she learns superrich Ares needs a wife, she proposes a deal: her freedom in exchange for marriage!

#4060 FORBIDDEN TO THE DESERT PRINCE
The Royal Desert Legacy
by Maisey Yates
If the sheikh wants Ariel, his promised bride, fiercely loyal Prince Cairo *will* deliver her. But the forbidden desire between them threatens *everything*. Her plans, his honor and the future of a nation!

HPCNMRA1022

#4061 THE CHRISTMAS HE CLAIMED THE SECRETARY
The Outrageous Accardi Brothers
by Caitlin Crews

To avoid an unwanted marriage of convenience, playboy Tiziano needs to manufacture a love affair with secretary Annie. Yet he's wholly unprepared for the wild heat between them—which he *must* attempt to restrain before it devours them both!

#4062 THE TWIN SECRET SHE MUST REVEAL
Scandals of the Le Roux Wedding
by Joss Wood

Thadie has not one but two reminders of those incredible hours in Angus's arms. But unable to contact her twins' elusive father, the society heiress decides she must move on. Until she's caught in a paparazzi frenzy and the security expert who rescues her is Angus himself!

#4063 WEDDING NIGHT WITH THE WRONG BILLIONAIRE
Four Weddings and a Baby
by Dani Collins

When her perfect-on-paper wedding ends in humiliation, Eden flees...with best man Remy! Their families' rivalry makes him *completely* off-limits. But when their attraction is red-hot, would claiming her wedding night with Remy be so very wrong?

#4064 A RING FOR THE SPANIARD'S REVENGE
by Abby Green

For self-made billionaire Vidal, nothing is out of reach. Except exacting revenge on Eva, whose family left a painful mark on his impoverished childhood. Until the now-penniless heiress begs for Vidal's help. He's prepared to agree...*if* she poses as his fiancée!

YOU CAN FIND MORE INFORMATION ON UPCOMING HARLEQUIN TITLES, FREE EXCERPTS AND MORE AT HARLEQUIN.COM.

SPECIAL EXCERPT FROM

⊕HARLEQUIN
PRESENTS

Read on for a sneak preview of
Dani Collins's next story for Harlequin Presents,
Wedding Night with the Wrong Billionaire

"It's just us here." The words slipped out of her, impetuous, desperate.

A distant part of her urged her to show some sense. She knew Micah would never forgive her for so much as getting in Remy's car, but they had had something in Paris. It had been interrupted, and the not knowing what could have been had left her with an ache of yearning that had stalled her in some way. If she couldn't have Remy, then it didn't matter who she married. They were all the same because they weren't him.

"No one would know."

"This would only be today. An hour. We couldn't tell anyone. Ever. If Hunter found out—"

"If Micah found out," she echoed with a catch in her voice. "I don't care about any of that, Remy. I really don't."

"After this, it goes back to the way it was, like we didn't even know one another. Is that really what you want?" His face twisted with conflict.

"No," she confessed with a chasm opening in her chest. "But I'll take it."

He closed his eyes, swearing as he fell back against the door with a defeated thump.

"Come here, then."

Don't miss
Wedding Night with the Wrong Billionaire.

Available December 2022 wherever
Harlequin Presents books and ebooks are sold.

Harlequin.com

Copyright © 2022 by Dani Collins

Get 4 FREE REWARDS!

We'll send you 2 FREE Books plus 2 FREE Mystery Gifts.

FREE Value Over **$20**

Both the **Harlequin® Desire** and **Harlequin Presents®** series feature compelling novels filled with passion, sensuality and intriguing scandals.

YES! Please send me 2 FREE novels from the Harlequin Desire or Harlequin Presents series and my 2 FREE gifts (gifts are worth about $10 retail). After receiving them, if I don't wish to receive any more books, I can return the shipping statement marked "cancel." If I don't cancel, I will receive 6 brand-new Harlequin Presents Larger-Print books every month and be billed just $6.05 each in the U.S. or $6.24 each in Canada, a savings of at least 10% off the cover price or 6 Harlequin Desire books every month and be billed just $4.80 each in the U.S. or $5.49 each in Canada, a savings of at least 13% off the cover price. It's quite a bargain! Shipping and handling is just 50¢ per book in the U.S. and $1.25 per book in Canada.* I understand that accepting the 2 free books and gifts places me under no obligation to buy anything. I can always return a shipment and cancel at any time by calling the number below. The free books and gifts are mine to keep no matter what I decide.

Choose one: ☐ **Harlequin Desire**
(225/326 HDN GRTW)

☐ **Harlequin Presents Larger-Print**
(176/376 HDN GQ9Z)

Name (please print)

Address   Apt. #

City   State/Province   Zip/Postal Code

Email: Please check this box ☐ if you would like to receive newsletters and promotional emails from Harlequin Enterprises ULC and its affiliates. You can unsubscribe anytime.

Mail to the **Harlequin Reader Service:**
IN U.S.A.: P.O. Box 1341, Buffalo, NY 14240-8531
IN CANADA: P.O. Box 603, Fort Erie, Ontario L2A 5X3

Want to try 2 free books from another series! Call 1-800-873-8635 or visit www.ReaderService.com.

*Terms and prices subject to change without notice. Prices do not include sales taxes, which will be charged (if applicable) based on your state or country of residence. Canadian residents will be charged applicable taxes. Offer not valid in Quebec. This offer is limited to one order per household. Books received may not be as shown. Not valid for current subscribers to the Harlequin Presents or Harlequin Desire series. All orders subject to approval. Credit or debit balances in a customer's account(s) may be offset by any other outstanding balance owed by or to the customer. Please allow 4 to 6 weeks for delivery. Offer available while quantities last.

Your Privacy—Your information is being collected by Harlequin Enterprises ULC, operating as Harlequin Reader Service. For a complete summary of the information we collect, how we use this information and to whom it is disclosed, please visit our privacy notice located at corporate.harlequin.com/privacy-notice. From time to time we may also exchange your personal information with reputable third parties. If you wish to opt out of this sharing of your personal information, please visit readerservice.com/consumerschoice or call 1-800-873-8635. **Notice to California Residents**—Under California law, you have specific rights to control and access your data. For more information on these rights and how to exercise them, visit corporate.harlequin.com/california-privacy.

HDHP22R2

IF YOU ENJOYED THIS BOOK
WE THINK YOU WILL ALSO LOVE

⬦ HARLEQUIN
DESIRE

Luxury, scandal, desire—welcome to
the lives of the American elite.

Be transported to the worlds of oil barons, family dynasties,
moguls and celebrities. Get ready for juicy plot twists,
delicious sensuality and intriguing scandal.

6 NEW BOOKS AVAILABLE EVERY MONTH!

HDXSERIES2021

HARLEQUIN

Heartfelt or thrilling, passionate or uplifting—Harlequin is more than just happily-ever-after.

With twelve different series to choose from and new books available every month, you are sure to find stories that will move you, uplift you, inspire and delight you.

SIGN UP FOR THE HARLEQUIN NEWSLETTER

Be the first to hear about great new reads and exciting offers!

Harlequin.com/newsletters

HNEWS2021